Gerri Russell

Published by Montlake Romance, Seattle

www.apub.com

Amazon, the Amazon logo, and Montlake Romance are trademarks of Amazon.com, Inc., or its affiliates.

ISBN-13: 9781503941557
ISBN-10: 1503941558

Cover design by Michael Rehder

Printed in the United States of America

With love and gratitude to April Rickard, who has cheered for my triumphs, wept for my sorrows, and enriched my life with her friendship. And to Pamela Bradburn, Teresa DesJardien, and Karen Harbaugh with equal parts admiration and love.

CHAPTER ONE

Ellie Hawthorne knew she'd done something terribly stupid last night. Just how stupid was the thousand-dollar question. That first shot of tequila had seemed like a good idea given the horrible day she'd had. Looking back, and judging by the pounding in her temples, Ellie was certain the second and third shots had been a mistake. Anything beyond that third shot, she didn't remember.

What had happened after that? Only snippets of memory played across her mind—dancing with a tall, blond man to a pulsing beat, pink peonies, white lace, Elvis Presley.

Was the memory some weird Vegas-induced fantasy?

Ellie groaned and rolled onto her side, away from the sliver of light stabbing through a separation in the curtains of her Las Vegas hotel room. She'd come to Vegas for an event-planning trade show, where she'd hoped to pick up potential clients for her ailing business.

Ellie Hawthorne Events hadn't had a long-term client since last spring, when her biggest celebrity wedding ever had canceled. The couple had opted for a homespun wedding instead, kicking off a new trend not only in Seattle but all over the nation. Event planners everywhere were struggling for work. And that reality had led to her first shot of tequila. And, she felt a shiver, maybe some other dumb decisions . . .

Something was knocking on her brain's back door.

In an attempt to stop the pounding in her head, Ellie pressed her hands against her temples. What *had* happened last night? She searched for any real memory that might surface. Again, she saw a man. He was handsome and somewhat familiar. He'd picked her up and carried her somewhere . . . nothing more came to her but the relentless throbbing.

Once again that thin streak of light assailed her. Why was the Las Vegas sun brighter than the one in Seattle? It didn't seem fair, especially with a killer hangover, that the sun should be so cheery.

Ellie groaned against the injustice of it all until that thought led to another. If she wanted to change her situation, she could. She could get up and find the aspirin she'd packed. What was that recipe for hangovers again? An aspirin, orange juice, and a raw egg? Her stomach roiled at the thought. She squeezed her eyes shut, hoping to stave off a wave of nausea. Dry toast sounded better. Maybe that *and* an aspirin.

Flipping the sheet aside on her king-size bed, she felt an air-conditioned chill settle over her bare skin. Funny, she didn't remember getting undressed last night. But she didn't remember coming back to her room either. Pushing herself to keep moving, she opened her eyes, then gasped at the sight of a man's head lying on the pillow next to hers.

Ellie jerked upright and scrambled out of bed. Her heart thundered in her ears, competing with the pounding in her head. For a moment her stomach pitched, and she thought she might be sick. She clamped her hand over her mouth. The sensation eased, and her eyes adjusted to the partial light.

A tall, blond man—the one from her memories—was very naked and in her bed. His slow, even breathing stopped. He stirred at the garbled sound that had escaped from her before settling back to sleep.

Should she call the front desk and ask for help? She dismissed the thought as quickly as it formed. He was no malicious stranger. Her fragmented memories indicated she'd invited him here.

Ellie forced herself to take a breath, then another as her heartbeat slowed. She reached for the sheet hanging off the edge of the bed. Wrapping the linen around her, she studied the man.

His back was to her, and he'd kicked off the remaining blankets, leaving her a clear view of the well-defined muscles of his back, waist, buttocks, and legs. Whoever he was, he was a sight to behold.

Ellie shook her head at the thought, then regretted the motion. She reached for the nightstand to steady herself. The body and the guy seemed so familiar. Yet no memories of his name or where they'd met came to her. How could she have forgotten such a finely sculpted posterior?

Her hand felt different. She turned her fingers, revealing the back of her left hand, which held the sheet to her body. Her breath hitched on a startled gasp. A big diamond sat atop her third finger.

The world seemed to slow down. A heaviness descended over her, weighing her down as her heartbeat thundered in her ears.

Was she . . . married?

There had to be an explanation. Ellie staggered toward the wall beside her, searching for the light. She flipped the switch and recoiled from the brightness. When her eyes adjusted, she looked again toward the bed. Blond hair lay against the white cotton of the pillow. "Wake up. Whoever you are, wake up!"

The man groaned and twisted onto his back, pulling the blanket with him, covering his lower half. He dragged his arm over his face, shielding his eyes from the light. "Too bright. Turn it off."

A day's growth of beard stubbled his square jaw and upper lip, giving him a roguish look that was a little more appealing than she cared to admit. No wonder her drunk self had been attracted to him. Looking farther down, she saw that his chest was broad and chiseled and covered with a smattering of golden hair. The man was definitely something to look at, but she needed to know more. She stepped toward the side of the bed, leaned down, and poked his shoulder. "Please. We need to talk."

His arm lifted, exposing his eyes. He gave her a devilish smile that held infinite promise. "Come back to bed. We can talk later." He patted the empty mattress beside him.

The sight of him rocked her. She hadn't looked into those dark-green eyes since high school. And that voice . . . her body had always responded to that deep, rich sound. An uncontrollable warmth spread through her. She hadn't seen him in eleven years. Even so, she could feel her nerves stretching in anticipation.

Never in her wildest dreams had she imagined herself this close to, and certainly not in bed with, the man who'd once broken her heart.

And yet she'd spent the night with him, or at least she thought she had. She vowed in that moment never to drink tequila again.

"Connor Grayson. What are you doing in my bed?"

Damn, he still looked good after all these years. In her fantasies, she'd hoped the next time she saw him he'd be bald and pudgy. Instead, Connor was handsome, muscular, and incredibly sexy, with not a gray hair in sight.

He blinked, then searched her face. After a long pause, his brows drew together as though he suddenly recognized her. "How in the hell did you get in my room?" His voice was no longer sexy, but hard.

"Your room? This is my room." At least she hoped it was. A quick glance at her hairbrush on the dresser left her not only dizzy but relieved that this truly was her room. Why had she brought him back into her life? He was not someone she trusted. So why were they together . . . like this?

As Connor appraised her from head to toe, Ellie pulled the sheet more tightly around herself. As she did, the unusual weight of the ring pulled at her finger. Had she indulged in more than a fling with Connor Grayson? Because not only was there a ring on her finger; he sported a shiny platinum band on his as well. "We did not get married last night," she said in a strangled tone, and she heard the doubt in her own voice.

◆ ◆ ◆

The last thing Connor Grayson had expected when he'd planned his trip to Las Vegas was to come face-to-face with his past. That past stared at him with wide, accusing eyes. If anyone should feel abused and irate in this situation, it should be him.

Eleven years ago Ellie Hawthorne had torn out his heart from his chest and ground it beneath her heel. Deep inside, where nothing and no one touched any longer, he still felt betrayed. And even though they both lived in Seattle, they'd never been in contact again after they'd graduated.

But why here and now? How had she known he'd be in Las Vegas? "Have you been spying on me?"

"What are you talking about?" Ellie asked, her voice sharp. "Did you not hear me?" She waved her finger beneath his nose. "Why am I wearing this ring? Why were we in bed together? What happened last night?" She asked her questions in a rush, then released a sharp breath and sagged down on the edge of the bed.

She raked her fingers through the wild tumble of burnished-gold locks he remembered oh so well.

"Oh God. Why did I have more than one drink last night?"

Connor didn't answer. He stared down at the platinum band around his ring finger. "What the hell? As if dating you in high school wasn't bad enough. A lifetime together would be torture." Connor tried to pull up even one memory from last night. How had he ended up with Ellie Hawthorne when every instinct in his body had been tuned to reject anyone like her?

The faint scent of wildflowers permeated his senses. He forced his thoughts away from the reminder of Ellie. He'd hated that scent ever since high school. He hated the way her presence lit up a room. Even standing still, Ellie had always had a vivaciousness that flowed through every line of her enticing form. Just a glimpse of her near or far used to set his heart racing. That his heart was now thumping in his chest in an unfamiliar rhythm was certainly not due to her. He decided to blame it on the shock of finding her in bed with him.

Still, he had to admit, she did look good after all these years. Her hair, which had always reminded him of spun gold, tumbled around her shoulders, framing her perfectly proportioned oval face with its high, chiseled cheekbones, large, almond-shaped eyes framed with thick lashes, and full and tempting lips.

Connor fisted his hands at his sides. So she was pretty. He was immune to her type. As though betraying that very thought, his groin tightened. His body's reaction released him from the spell of her charms. She'd always had this effect on him in the past. Obviously the present was no different. He had to put some distance between them. Then he could be his usual logical self and find the perspective he needed.

He stood, allowing the blanket to fall to his feet, exposing himself, fully aroused, to her while he grabbed a pair of pants that lay abandoned on the floor. Tuxedo pants.

She looked away, focusing on the creamy-white dress on the floor at the end of the bed. She picked up the garment, which had been abandoned in a heap. "We *did* get married last night!"

"This clothing doesn't prove anything," Connor said, more harshly than he'd intended. The look on her face was one of disgust, not joy or acceptance.

"Wedding rings, wedding clothes . . . it's getting harder to think otherwise." She dropped the gown, allowing it to fall in a puddle on the floor. She turned away, toward the bedside, searching for something. When she located her cell phone, she swiped the screen, then turned back to him with wide, almost horrified eyes. "Look."

On the screen he saw a picture of the two of them locked in each other's arms, standing between two men dressed very much like Elvis Presley. "Is that a joke?"

"It looks pretty real to me." Ellie sagged against the dresser. "So did we *just* get married, or did we get married and have sex?"

Connor frowned. Why did she have to look so horrified at the thought of them having sex? "You don't remember anything about last night?"

"I remember snippets. I thought it was all some strange tequila-induced nightmare. Do you remember anything about Elvis?"

"Presley? He's dead."

"Not in Vegas."

Connor blew out a breath as he reached for his crumpled tuxedo shirt, pulling it over his head without bothering to undo the buttons. "I knew coming to Vegas was a bad idea."

"That's an understatement." Ellie bent to the floor and retrieved a lacy pair of black bikini underwear and a bra near the wedding dress. "I wore black underwear with a white dress?" She winced as she tucked her undergarments in her palm, hiding them from his view. "Hang on. It's disturbing talking to you with only a sheet covering me." She hurried to the closet, reaching for a black dress with white polka dots, then slipped into the bathroom and locked the door.

"Maybe we should head back to the bar where we were last night? Someone there must remember something," he said loud enough that she could hear him through the door.

"That would be great. Do you remember the name of the bar?" she asked, emerging from the bathroom.

"No. I hoped you might." The words stuck in his throat. Her dress had looked so innocent on the hanger. On Ellie the garment sent his pulse racing. The open back exposed the lower half of her spine and hinted at the soft curves hidden just beneath the fabric at her waist. The short length exposed the one part of Ellie that had always left him feeling slightly breathless—her long, shapely legs. "Do you have to wear that dress?" He ground his teeth and forced his attention away.

Ellie's gaze narrowed. "What's wrong with my dress?"

"Damn," he said, releasing a heavy sigh. "Never mind."

Ellie's look turned puzzled, and he didn't blame her confusion. He knew the heated look he gave her didn't match his words.

"As soon as I find my socks and shoes, I'm going downstairs. I say we start there." Before he could search for the lost items, a knock sounded on the door. Startled, he opened the door to find four aging Elvis impersonators behind a room-service cart.

"How are our favorite newlyweds today?" asked an Elvis wearing a black wig and a white suit covered with rhinestones.

Ellie's eyes went wide. "A white Elvis? I didn't dream it. It really happened." Her face paled. "We are married. We're really, really, married."

White Elvis smiled, ignoring Ellie's obvious distress. "That you are."

"All of you were there? You witnessed us getting married?" Connor asked as a wave of disbelief washed over him.

The white Elvis nodded. "You were married at what everyone calls the Elvis Chapel. Best place in Vegas to tie the knot."

"We brought breakfast. After last night, you should eat something solid," said a blue Elvis, who stepped out from behind a red Elvis.

The eldest-looking of the bunch was an Elvis dressed in a gold lamé jacket worn over a black shirt and pants. He smiled apologetically. "To be honest, we're checking in on you two. You both had a lot to drink last night."

All four men were obviously well past Elvis's prime, being at least as old as Connor's own grandmother. Even so, with their stage makeup and false hair, Connor was sure the men could convincingly pass as Elvis impersonators at any Vegas show.

Blue Elvis grabbed two full glasses off the tray and strode past Connor into the room. "Try this. The contents will help shake off the effects of last night."

"What is it?" Ellie asked as he handed her the tall glass filled with a curiously orange liquid.

"My mama's secret hangover recipe. One part orange juice, one part beer, one part seltzer, and two crushed aspirin dissolved into the mix." Blue Elvis pushed the glass into her hand. "Go on—give it a try," he said with a twang that sounded very much like Elvis Presley.

When Ellie accepted the glass and brought it to her lips, Blue Elvis turned to Connor and offered him the same concoction. Connor didn't hesitate; he stepped aside, allowing the others to enter as he knocked the glass's contents back. He would try just about anything to greet this moment with a clearer head.

Blue Elvis remained beside Connor, while the other three removed the warming lids from the breakfast tray. Instantly the smell of bacon and maple syrup curled in the air.

"What is all this? Did we have the foresight to order breakfast last night when we can't remember much else?" Connor asked, surprised his stomach didn't lurch. Instead, it grumbled.

"Oh, no, young man. You had only one thing on your mind last night after we brought you both back to this room," White Elvis said, smiling like a satisfied cat.

Gold Elvis turned to a blushing Ellie and took her now-empty glass. "We were so honored the two of you asked us to be in your wedding that we wanted to come over today and make sure everything was all right."

"It was a beautiful ceremony," White Elvis said with a flourish of his hand that sent the red gussets in his sleeves flapping. "You two were insistent that the wedding begin at midnight." Glancing at Ellie, he said, "And all the little touches you added, like the crystals you laced through the flowers on the wedding bower, and the rose petals you arranged on the floor leading up to the altar, turned your wedding into a real classy event."

The color in Ellie's cheeks faded, and she swayed on her feet.

Rather than let her fall to the floor, Connor drew Ellie against his side, tucking his arm about her waist. She didn't resist.

Gold Elvis reached inside his jacket and removed a thin stack of photos. "Here's the proof. Your commemorative Elvis pics."

The man handed the pictures to Ellie. Connor looked on as she flipped through the evidence of their union.

Her face paled, and she stepped out of Connor's embrace. "We got married at the Chapel of Burning Love on Las Vegas Boulevard?"

"You were a handsome couple," Red Elvis said, drawing out the words.

"How did we get our wedding clothes?" she asked, her voice thin.

"The chapel has dresses, tuxes, flowers, and rings right there. The two of you only took a few minutes deciding. It appeared you were in a hurry to get down that aisle," Red Elvis said with a hearty laugh.

"I stood in as your Elvis of honor," Gold Elvis said, giving her a shy look as he took Ellie's hand and gave it a squeeze. "'Twas truly an honor."

Blue Elvis handed Connor an official-looking piece of paper from the cart. It was a wedding license bearing his own signature right next to what he assumed was Ellie's. "If you still need proof about what transpired between you and Ellie, here it is."

Ellie remained perfectly still, her face as pale as Connor had ever seen. But he didn't miss the temper building in the depths of her brown eyes.

"As a licensed minister, I married you two," Red Elvis continued proudly.

"Why would I do any of this?" Ellie asked as her temper suddenly broke free. "The most important day of my life, a day I've dreamed about since I was twelve." Her pitch rose with every word. "And I married him, of all people, in a themed chapel in Vegas with Elvis as my bridesmaid?" She threw the pictures of their wedding on the breakfast tray.

"Why are you the one who's pissed?" Connor objected as Ellie headed past him through the door.

All four of the older men looked stricken. "We didn't mean to upset either of you," Red Elvis said as Connor rushed past him.

"I told you we should have waited," Blue Elvis muttered. "Hangovers tend to make people less rational."

Ellie kept moving down the hallway.

"Where are you going?" Connor asked, following her to the elevators in his bare feet. He reached for her arm, then stopped himself.

She punched the "Call" button before turning to face him. Tears welled in her eyes. "I've got to figure this out. Why would I marry you? Why would you marry me?"

This time he didn't hold back. He reached for her, gently placing his hand on her wrist. "We need to figure this out. Together."

The elevator doors opened. She stepped inside. "You and I have caused each other enough pain already. What we need to figure out is how to get divorced in Vegas as quickly as we got married." The doors shut, leaving Connor to stare at his reflection in the shiny metal.

Get divorced? He hadn't even come to terms with the fact they were married, and she was talking about divorce? He shook his head at the odd thought. Of course she wanted to be rid of him every bit as much as he wanted to be rid of her. He did want to be rid of her, right?

Connor made his way back to Ellie's room. As soon as he pulled on his socks and shoes, he'd go after her. In the past, Ellie would have returned to the place where they'd started down this path. The woman he'd confronted this morning would no doubt do the same, searching for a reason or a memory that might help her understand why they'd married.

CHAPTER TWO

Connor walked through the open hotel room door to find all four Elvises standing right where he'd left them near the breakfast cart. Each held one of the pictures of his and Ellie's wedding in their hands.

White Elvis looked up and gave Connor a sad smile. "We've seen a lot of couples come through our chapel. You two seemed genuine about tying the knot forever."

Connor moved past them, searching for his socks and shoes, finding them under the bed. He should probably change out of the tuxedo he wore, but all his other clothes were in his own room somewhere in this gigantic hotel. He'd look ridiculous wearing a tuxedo at ten o'clock in the morning. But then again, in Vegas pretty much anything was acceptable at any time of day. "Sorry, guys. I need to leave."

Blue Elvis smiled, his eyes crinkling at the corners. "You're going after her, aren't you?"

Before Connor could answer, his cell phone chimed. He withdrew the device from the pocket of his pants. He looked at the screen, hoping it was Ellie even though he had no idea if she knew his cell number. Maybe they'd exchanged them last night along with all the other things neither of them could remember.

Instead of Ellie, his father's phone number appeared on the screen. Why would his dad call him now? He knew he'd be busy with the trials for his self-driving car. Or at least he would have been had the onboard computer not failed.

Connor answered the call even though he had no time to talk. "Hey, Dad. Can I call you back in an hour?"

"No time for that." His father's voice vibrated with urgency.

A cold chill slithered down Connor's spine. "What's wrong?"

"Your grandmother Viola had a heart attack last night. Things don't look good," Clark Grayson informed his son somberly. "She's headed into bypass surgery this morning and asked to see her only grandson when she wakes up. Please come home. Your grandmother needs you."

Connor took a steadying breath. There was no time for emotion. He could fall apart later. Right now his grandmother needed him. "I'll be there as soon as I can catch the next plane, Dad. Tell Grandmother I'll see her soon."

"Everything okay?" Red Elvis asked when Connor ended the call.

"I've got to go." Connor looked around in a daze for a moment until it dawned on him that he was still in Ellie's room. "Ellie," Connor said, her name booming in the silence that had fallen.

He had to get to the airport. He also had to go after his *temporary* bride.

"Can we help at all?" Red Elvis asked. "Sounds like something at home isn't quite right."

"My grandmother had a heart attack. I need to get back to Seattle." Connor said the words, but his mind was already working on how to be in two places at once and how to deal with this awkward situation with Ellie.

He heard the four Elvises mumble something to one another as he hurriedly pulled on his socks and slammed his feet into his shoes. The last conversation he'd had with his grandmother before he'd left for Las Vegas played through his mind. She'd teased him, saying, "I want to live long enough to see you settled down."

In that moment, he felt a quiver of hope as a crazy plan began to take shape.

Marriage was important to Viola. She'd be so happy to know he'd married. It was all she ever talked about when Connor visited her every Sunday. What if . . . he really was married? Maybe that would give his grandmother something to live for. He'd heard stories of people overcoming the greatest odds if they had a strong enough incentive.

But what about Ellie? Could he convince her to fly back to Seattle with him? And then would she pose as his bride until his grandmother either recovered enough to handle the news that they would divorce or until she . . . Connor couldn't finish the thought.

His grandmother would live. That was the only eventuality he would focus on. And he was willing to do anything to see that happen, even if it meant staying tied to the one woman he'd vowed never to let into his life again.

◆ ◆ ◆

Lenny, George, Ernie, and Aaron waited in silence for Connor to leave the room. The moment he did, Lenny wilted onto the bed even though he knew his red costume clashed with the gold bedspread. You never knew when a photo op would occur, and he was usually hyperaware of putting himself to his best advantage. At the moment, though, he didn't really care. "Oh dear, not Viola."

George paled, suddenly serious as his cheeks took on a similar pallor to the white costume he wore. "Our girl is sick."

"She's not our girl anymore," Aaron interjected, though worry hung in his words. "I wish she was."

"She'll always be our girl," Ernie said with a sigh.

"You're right," the others agreed.

Lenny's thoughts moved to the past. Along with Viola, the five of them had been a late-night lounge act in the 1950s at the Sands Hotel alongside entertainment greats such as Tony Bennett, Frank Sinatra, Dean Martin, and Judy Garland.

The two years they were together had been the best of their lives. Then in an unexpected turn of events, Viola quit the group to marry a man she'd met the week before. The four of them had continued on as a musical act, but nothing was ever the same without Viola.

It wasn't until 1977 when Elvis Presley died that the four of them truly bounced back—this time as Elvis impersonators. Viola had stayed in touch and was thrilled that they'd made a comeback in the entertainment world. Yet not one of them had married, as each only had a place in his heart for one girl: Viola.

Lenny pushed back his fear. He had to be strong for all of them—including Viola. "Remember that song Viola used to sing . . . 'Nothing's Going to Keep Me from You'?"

Ernie's lips pulled up in a sentimental smile. "That was her signature song."

"When she wrote that song, she wrote it for all of us, for everything we were together," Lenny reminded his friends.

"You're right," George agreed in an unusually serious voice. "Viola will be okay. She has to be, especially now that we finally helped her get her heart's desire."

"I don't know," Aaron said with an Elvis shake of his false black hair. Beneath that wig he was the baldest of the bunch. "Ellie didn't look too happy about her current situation. I heard her say the word *divorce* before the elevator closed."

George stomped his foot, sending the red gusset in his white pant leg flapping. "Connor's marriage can't end that way. What happened here in Vegas between them . . . it has to mean something."

Lenny looked at the men around him, his gaze going from face to face. "Ellie and Connor may need our help realizing what they've been given. We owe it to Viola."

If there was anything the four of them liked better than impersonating Elvis, it was helping the misguided find their way. Lenny's heart beat a little faster. The cold that had settled inside him in response to the news of Viola's condition faded, replaced by an overflowing warmth that filled the corners of his aging soul.

Aaron tugged at the edge of his blue jacket as a flicker of pain crossed his face. "Viola's been on her own for a long time now."

"She won't be alone any longer. We have a new mission, my friends. We're going to Seattle. We'll make sure Viola knows we're near, but we'll also make certain our newlyweds don't make a mistake they'll regret for the rest of their lives."

Ernie plunged his hands into the pockets of his gold lamé jacket. "We can't force them to stay together."

Lenny narrowed his gaze. "Who said anything about force?"

"Have you learned nothing from playing Elvis for almost forty years?" George wiggled his bushy brows. "Some things aren't meant to die."

"Ain't that the truth," Lenny exclaimed as they strode out of the hotel room and toward the elevator with their Elvis personas once again in place.

◆ ◆ ◆

Because of traffic on the Las Vegas Strip, the drive to the Chapel of Burning Love seemed to take forever. Connor parked his rental car around the back of the small white building. As he walked along the sidewalk to the arched front doors, the building suddenly seemed vaguely familiar.

Memories tiptoed across his mind as he stepped into the foyer. He remembered sweeping Ellie off her feet and carrying her across the threshold. He'd had no idea which threshold he was supposed to carry her over, so he'd carried her over every single one from the chapel to the hotel to her hotel room.

And he remembered her smile. At the start of their evening together as they took that first drink of tequila, her smile had been too stiff to be real, too forced. She hadn't been pleased to see him, and he knew he certainly hadn't wanted to see her despite their paths crossing once again.

It was what he'd seen in her eyes after the second and third shots of tequila that had made him stay in the chair beside her—her desperate loneliness, her fragile self-worth. Those emotions had echoed in his own soul, had helped him set aside their past for the moment as he offered her his hand for a dance.

Shaking his head to clear the memory, Connor stepped through the chapel doorway. He found Ellie in the small room, sitting at the altar, staring at a wooden bower covered in artificial white roses and strands of crystals where they'd said their vows.

His heart hammered in his chest as he approached her, as he remembered the way she'd looked at him last night. The way her gaze had connected with his. The way her false smile faded as a real one took its place.

At the altar he stopped and waited for her to register his presence. Slowly she turned toward him. He released his breath, not realizing he'd been holding it.

"How did you know where to find me?" she asked with a fleeting smile. Definitely not the same one as last night.

"It was the only logical place," he replied, searching for a way to ask what he needed to ask.

"I still can't figure it out . . . why did we get married?" Ellie asked quietly.

"We can blame it on the tequila. Or we can spend a little time figuring out the reasons," he replied, moving closer to her.

"You want to figure out why we got married?" she asked, not quite meeting his eyes.

"Don't you?"

Ellie looked back at the wedding bower. It was a long minute before she spoke again, and when she did, her voice was strained. "I used to believe in happily ever after. I'm not sure I do anymore."

Connor frowned as he sat down beside her. "You're a wedding planner." He remembered at least that much of their conversation last night. "Isn't believing in such things a requirement for you?"

"I'm an event planner. I do more than weddings." She turned back to him but didn't meet his gaze. "Even so, I've planned so many weddings for other people that were exquisite—a fantasy come true for the bride and groom. Some of those couples are still together; some aren't. It's the ones who focused on their lives after the wedding and not on the wedding itself that made it as a couple."

"You had a fantasy wedding," Connor said. "It's not every day that Elvis marries a couple."

Ellie screwed up her face. "I'm pretty sure that happens in Vegas every day, especially in this chapel. Or do you not remember our wedding photos?"

"I remember." He allowed silence to slip between them before he continued. "The fact is, we *are* married. And before we do anything to change that state, I need to ask you a favor."

"What kind of favor?" she asked. Her eyes filled with suspicion. "What could you possibly want from me?"

"My father called me after you left the hotel. My grandmother has had a heart attack. She's having surgery today. Even so, my father says her prognosis isn't good. He asked me to come home quickly. In case she . . ." He couldn't say the word.

With concern in her eyes, Ellie faced him. "I'm so sorry, Connor. I only met your grandmother a few times, but I could tell she was someone special."

"Would you stay married to me for a little while longer?" he asked softly. He watched her face, waiting for a response. His heart beat a little faster. His palms grew damp. Time was of the essence here. He needed her to say yes.

"Stay married? To you?"

"Yes. Viola has said to me more than once that she wanted to live long enough to see me married. I can't let her down." He took Ellie's hands in his own. "Will you come back to Seattle with me as my bride for my grandmother's sake? Let's pretend we're happy together, at least while my grandmother recovers. Once she's better, I'll give you the divorce you want." He couldn't let his grandmother die without her at least believing he had found his one and only—like she had found his grandfather. If she recovered, he would find a way to explain what he'd done to try to keep her alive.

"Will you do it?" Connor asked.

The color faded from Ellie's cheeks. "You want us to stay married for your grandmother's sake?" Her eyes hardened. "It would be a lie."

The words twisted inside him, but he pushed aside the memories that threatened. "My grandmother needs something to encourage her to fight for her life. Please, Ellie. I'm not ready to let her go just yet."

"You really think our marriage will give her something to live for?" The glimmer of compassion in her eyes filled him with hope.

"Yes."

Ellie pushed a lock of hair away from her face. "And when we tell her the truth? You think she'll be better off knowing we lied to her then?"

"She'll be alive at least. I can deal with the rest," Connor replied.

Ellie closed her eyes, hiding her emotions from him. When she opened them a moment later, their brown depths were clear and expressionless. "I need to ask you something, Connor. Something that has nothing to do with your grandmother."

"Okay," he said, suddenly curious.

She opened the small purse at her side and withdrew a handful of hundred-dollar bills. "We didn't gamble last night, did we?"

He shook his head, remembering the stack of bills he'd given her. He also remembered the radiance of her smile when he'd placed them in her hand.

"You gave these to me, didn't you?"

He nodded. "I found it very admirable, what you're doing."

"Why support me in that way?" In that moment, she looked at him through the eyes he remembered.

"When you told me about the Birthday Project, you looked so sad because you didn't have the funds to continue for October. I had the money, so I gave it to you," he said with what he hoped was a casual shrug.

"Do you still feel the same way today, now that the thrill of last night and all the tequila are gone?" she asked, holding the money out to him.

He curled his hand around hers, gently guiding her hand and the money back toward her purse. "I still think what you're doing is noble, and I'm happy to sponsor this month's party."

She stared at the money a moment longer before returning it to her purse. "I started the Birthday Project because of a little boy. He couldn't have been more than five, strolling through Pike Place Market in front of me. He reached out and stole an apple from one of the vendors, then raced off. Before the vendor could chase him down, I paid for the apple, then followed the boy myself. I found him a few blocks away, hunched down in an alley, holding the apple before him and singing the birthday song to himself. When he saw me, he started to run, but I talked him into staying. We sat in that alley for a long time, talking about all the homeless kids, like himself, whose parents can't celebrate their birthdays in any notable way given their circumstances. In that moment, I vowed I'd find a way to change that. To help kids like Kevin feel recognized and loved."

She looked up at Connor, meeting his gaze. "Thank you for helping me keep my promise for October. It means the world to me and to the kids it will help."

Connor could only nod, owing to the tightness in his throat.

Her expression softened. "All right. You helped me. I'll help you. When do we leave?" Her words were only a thread above a whisper.

Connor forced back his own response to her story and looked at his watch. "I already called the airlines. Our flight leaves in two hours. We have just enough time to get back to the hotel for our things and then return my rental car before our flight."

She frowned. "You were that sure I'd agree to your plan?"

He shrugged. "I hoped."

She tipped her chin. Defiance radiated from her every pore. "Yeah, keep making assumptions about me, Grayson, and this arrangement won't last very long," she said, walking away from him, down the aisle toward the door.

After a few seconds he caught up with her. "It won't happen again." He tossed the apology out there like it meant something; then he realized that it really did. He needed her help. There was really nothing for her to gain from this arrangement except his cooperation with a quick divorce.

Connor took her hand.

She started to pull away.

He held tight. "We might as well start practicing now if we're going to convince my grandmother we're a couple."

Ellie released a sigh. "This really wasn't what I had planned when I came to Las Vegas."

Connor forced back a flippant response. "What were you hoping to accomplish?" he asked instead, certain they'd never discussed why either of them was in town last night.

"I was looking for clients for my business," she said as they made their way to the parking lot.

"I'll hire you."

She pulled her hand from his. "To do what?"

He shrugged. "I'll need a launch party for my latest robotics project in the next few months if all goes well."

"That won't help me right now—besides, I'm not sure it's wise to complicate our situation further, Grayson."

At the moment, and in that tone of voice, she made his name sound like a curse. The thought rattled him as he opened the car door for her. She had been the curse of his life, not the other way around.

They had met the beginning of their senior year in high school because Ellie had needed a tutor for calculus. Sequestered in the library each day after school, the geek and the cheerleader became friends, allowing each to see who the other truly was despite the social pressure from their peers.

Connor hadn't let anyone get too close after his mother disappeared from his life. But Ellie was different. Special. She didn't dismiss him as a nerd like everybody else seemed to, and she truly cared for him. After four months of dating, things got serious. They'd planned to attend different colleges on opposite coasts, yet they wanted to make a lasting commitment to each other. Prom would have been the night, except that plan hadn't gone as expected.

Old, painful memories flooded back as he settled into the car beside her. He told himself he didn't blame her for leaving him behind. They'd been so young—young enough to lie to themselves about their future. Over the years he'd convinced himself their breakup had been for the best. They would have ruined each other's lives, suffocated each other's dreams.

But in this moment, staring at her in the front seat of his car, he realized he hadn't forgiven her. How could he? She'd abandoned him just like his mother had. Aside from his grandmother, every other woman he'd allowed into his heart had let him down.

Ellie Hawthorne might not be the girl he once fell in love with, but she was the best hope for saving his grandmother's life.

CHAPTER THREE

"Here we go," Connor said outside the door of his grandmother's small ICU room at Swedish Hospital on Seattle's Capitol Hill.

The words grated on Ellie's overly sensitive nerves as she and Connor stepped into the room. She'd agreed to this scheme. There was no turning back now.

Connor's grandmother lay as still as death on the narrow bed. No wonder Connor had been so eager to get to the hospital as soon as they'd landed at Sea-Tac Airport. Viola Grayson's eyes were closed. The railed sides of the bed made the woman in between look so frail and small, with the covers tucked up under her chin. Several bags hung from a metal pole beside the bed, sending a long line of clear tubing into the back of her hand.

The gray-haired woman looked serene, as though she hadn't a care in the world. Ellie kept an easy smile in place even as her heart climbed in her throat. They'd been allowed to see Viola for only a few minutes to share their good news . . . or their lie, depending on how you looked at the situation.

The electronic drone of the cardiac monitor filled the confines of the small room. A glance at the man beside her revealed he was keeping his emotions in check, but she didn't miss the tightness of his breath or the slight sheen of moisture in his eyes. His worry was palpable.

Unable to stop herself, Ellie reached out and took his hand. He hesitated, then gripped her hand firmly, as though he needed her strength for what came next.

"Grandmother?" Connor said in a warm, soothing voice as they stopped beside the bed. "I'd like you to meet my wife."

They waited breathlessly for her to open her eyes.

At first she didn't respond, she just lay there, breathing. Ellie lifted her gaze to the cardiac monitor. A green line danced across the screen, its peaks and dips in a regular rhythm. She didn't know much about hearts or heart surgery, but the line looked steady and normal.

Two beeps later, Viola's eyelashes fluttered, and she opened her eyes. The older woman turned toward the sound of Connor's voice. "Your . . . wife?" The words were soft, strained, yet a hint of joy hung in her tone.

Ellie and Connor were here to urge the older woman to fight harder, to live for the future. Tears spilled down Ellie's cheeks, not because Viola had responded in a positive way but at the relief she could feel in Connor's grip on her hand. He lifted Ellie's fingers to his lips and pressed a kiss to her knuckles. A tingle of sensation rippled down her arm.

"She's going to be fine," Connor said, turning to face Ellie, giving her a dazzling smile. The smile was all part of the show they were performing for his grandmother's sake, yet it still did strange things to her insides.

The emotion of the moment made her feel light-headed and nauseated at the same time. Ellie took a breath, clearing the sensations, then turned to the woman on the bed. She must play her part.

Ellie didn't remember much about Viola from her high school days except that the woman always seemed to rule everyone around her with an iron fist in a velvet glove. "Hello, Viola. It's nice to see you again." What an inane and ordinary thing to say to a dying woman who was now technically her grandmother-in-law.

Viola didn't seem to care as she looked up at both her and Connor. "Did I hear you right?" she asked in a weak voice. "Are you married?"

"We are," Ellie said at the same time as Connor.

"It's all I've ever wanted for my grandson," Viola said, her voice growing stronger. Tears rolled down the sides of her cheeks. "Weren't you in Las Vegas this week, Connor?"

Connor nodded. "Ellie was in Vegas as well, looking for clients for her event-planning company. Our paths crossed." He sent Ellie a heated look before turning back to his grandmother. "And we were so swept away with emotion, we couldn't wait to marry."

Joy filled her expression as she stared up at them. "It's like my prayers have been answered."

Connor patted his grandmother's hand. "Don't you worry about anything other than getting better. Ellie and I will be here to help."

Viola's eyes drifted closed, as though talking was taking everything out of her. "You're newlyweds. You need time to yourselves."

"We're going to let you sleep, Grandmother."

The older woman's eyes snapped open. "Not yet. Please. Where will you live? Surely not at that small condominium of yours, Connor."

Connor bent over and touched her face, gently stroking her velvety wrinkles. "We haven't discussed our living arrangements yet. We were in a hurry to get home to see you."

Disrupting the perfection of the sheets, Viola brought her frail, age-spotted hand to cover his. "It's settled then. You'll move into my house."

"No, Grandmother," Connor said. "We couldn't do that. It's *your* house."

"I haven't lived at Grayson House for years. The old house is in need of a few repairs that are well beyond my ability to oversee."

"What kind of repairs?" Connor asked. "Why didn't you ask for help?"

"I didn't want to bother anyone." Suddenly seeming too tired to hold her hand up, she dropped it at her side.

Connor's face paled, visibly shaken by the woman's weakness. "I'll do anything to help you, Grandmother."

"Good. Then move into the house."

Connor frowned. "My condo might be small, but your old Victorian is too big for the two of us."

"You said Ellie needed clients for her event-planning business." Viola might be weak, but her voice remained firm.

"Oh, it's fine, really. I'll find something soon," Ellie said past the lump that lodged in her throat. The woman was very ill, yet Ellie could see that iron fist coming out.

Viola's watery gaze passed between the two of them. "I was contacted last week about getting Grayson House ready for a holiday event—the Historical Society's Holiday Street of Dreams. I was going to turn it down. Getting the house ready would have been too much work for me to oversee. Now it all seems the perfect solution. Grayson House will be a place for you both to live, and the event will help Ellie until she finds more work."

Viola paused as she searched their faces. Her gaze narrowed. "Consider it helping to fulfill a dying woman's last wish."

Ellie pressed her lips together, holding back a gasp at the emotional blackmail. Viola might be sick, even dying, but she wanted their cooperation. Would Connor hold his ground or let Viola get her way?

"Grandmother," Connor said, his spine stiffening, "Ellie can't do that job alone. You said yourself that the house needs repairs. It's unfair to ask her to do such a thing."

"I'll hire you both."

Connor shook his head. "I already have a job that keeps me insanely busy. Besides, you need to focus on getting better. Not fixing up Grayson House."

"I want the house fixed up," she countered with a lift of her chin. Her cardiac monitor beeped a little faster. The green line spiked higher than it had before. "Knowing you both are doing the work will help me get better faster. Besides, you won't have to do that work by yourselves. Your grandfather left me oodles of money. You can hire whoever you want to help you."

Connor's gaze shifted from the monitor to his grandmother. His posture relaxed, and Ellie knew he was buckling. "When is this event supposed to take place?"

"The day after Thanksgiving."

"That's five weeks from now. I'd have to see the job to know if that schedule is workable," Ellie interjected, unable to keep silent a moment longer.

"I'm confident you can handle the challenge and the time frame," Viola said. "I'll pay each of you a salary. And, Connor, I'll make a sizable donation to the development of your self-driving car. That should allow you to hire others to assist you at the university and give you time to help Ellie with the house."

"That's very generous, Grandmother."

"You're my only grandson. I want to see you happy and successful." Viola started to say more, but then a phlegmy cough rattled through her chest.

Connor took his grandmother's hand, so slim and fragile, and squeezed it gently until the coughing subsided. The erratic beep of the machine beside her settled into a more stable pattern.

"I'm getting tired," Viola managed after a moment. "No more arguments. You know where the spare key is, Connor. Let yourselves in."

"We will," Connor agreed as he pulled up the sheets beneath her chin once more.

"Thank you," Viola said as she shut her eyes, sinking into the mattress.

"It's time for us to go and let you rest." Connor placed a final kiss on her forehead. "We'll talk more tomorrow."

While Ellie was relieved to have a new job, she didn't like the fact that Viola had manipulated her and Connor into living together for the next five weeks. The two of them would discuss a way around that situation as soon as they were out of earshot of Viola's room. Ellie followed after Connor to the edge of the nurse's station. She turned to face him only to meet Jordan Krane's quizzical gaze behind his shoulder.

Jordan had been Ellie's friend since high school. She knew, better than anyone, how the breakup with Connor had affected every relationship Ellie had had since. She also knew Ellie had vowed never to allow herself to be hurt by the man again . . .

They'd been high school sweethearts and each other's first love. She'd opened her heart and soul to him. Couldn't imagine a life without him. But he'd abandoned the dreams they'd forged at the first opportunity, thinking only of himself. He'd killed a part of her that year—a part he'd claimed to love. A part she'd never gotten back.

What are you doing with Connor Grayson? Jordan mouthed silently, her green eyes wide.

Jordan usually worked in the emergency room at Swedish Hospital as a physician's assistant. What was she doing in the ICU today?

"I'm sorry about my grandmother's insistence that we move in together," Connor said, unaware of Jordan behind him. "It only makes sense now that we're married."

"Move in together?" Jordan asked, no longer silent. She spun Connor around. "Married?" A tangled mix of horror and hysteria flashed through her eyes as she looked past him to Ellie. "What the hell? You don't even like him."

Surprise flickered across his features before he shuttered his gaze. "That's not how I interpreted things in Vegas."

"You were in Vegas together?" Jordan asked.

"Yes. No." Ellie stumbled over the words. "We bumped into each other there."

Jordan's eyes narrowed. "And got married?"

Ellie cast another glance at Connor. He searched her face as though he expected her to say something flippant. Instead, she calmly said, "Yes." Their marriage was between the two of them. No one else.

"Damn, girl. Don't you learn from your mistakes?" Jordan asked.

"He's not a mistake." The words erupted from her before she could stop them. What had happened between them was unfortunate, but she still wouldn't call Connor a mistake. She knew what it felt like to be considered as such. She wouldn't put that sense of worthlessness on another human being no matter how much he might have hurt her in the past.

Silence fell among them, punctuated only by the rhythmic whirring and beeping of medical monitors from the ICU rooms just beyond.

Jordan threw Ellie a questioning glance just as her pager beeped. "All right. I'll give you a reprieve for now because I have to respond to this, but you better be prepared to talk to Olivia and me on girls' night. See you Tuesday." With those words, Jordan left the two of them alone.

Ellie turned to Connor. "Don't mind Jordan. She can be a little blunt at times."

"Sounded like she knew what she was talking about." Irritation flashed in his expression.

Ellie opened her mouth to speak, but he stopped her by holding up his hand. "It doesn't matter how we feel about each other. Do we still have a deal? Will you stay married and live with me in Viola's house as my wife until she recovers?"

The job Viola offered was more than Ellie had ever dreamed possible. Viola might have been a bit manipulative in getting them to live in her house, but the Historical Society's Holiday Street of Dreams was a huge event in Seattle. Locals and visitors came from all over the country to see glorious houses from another era.

Ellie couldn't deny the sense of satisfaction that filled her at the thought that she would be a part of the event. She would have work again, and with that work she could proceed with her Birthday Project. And it would buy her time—time to figure out what came next.

For the next five weeks she'd have an income and something quite spectacular to accomplish. Given the desperation that had driven her to

Las Vegas, she was more than ready for the task of resurrecting Viola's old house. "Let's go to Grayson House. No time like the present to see what we're up against."

Had there ever been any truer words?

The next five weeks could be heaven or hell. It was time to find out which awaited them at Viola's old Victorian.

◆ ◆ ◆

As soon as Connor and Ellie disappeared around the corner and onto the hospital elevator, Aaron signaled for the boys to come out of the waiting room. Over the years, he'd become the group's self-appointed expert in subterfuge. Even though Connor and Ellie might not recognize them out of their Elvis costumes, they didn't want to chance being seen by the newlyweds.

"All clear," Aaron announced. George, Ernie, and Lenny joined him. Silently they crept toward Viola's room.

Code blue, ICU . . . Code blue. An alarm blared through the paging system, and a flurry of medical staff flew past them to a room down the hall. When the chaos cleared, the four men slipped into Viola's room unnoticed.

When Aaron saw Viola, he felt as if he were doing a free fall into a deep, dark hole. She looked dead. Gray and withered and still. So unlike the Viola they knew and loved. Aaron reached for the rails of her bed to steady himself. This wasn't how he'd imagined them seeing each other again after all these years.

Beside him the cardiac monitor beeped relentlessly, keeping time with his own thundering heartbeat. *No, I can do this,* Aaron encouraged himself. He had to be strong for Viola's sake. He straightened and forced a smile. "Hey there, sugar." It was the name he'd always called her.

Her eyes drifted open. "Aaron Peterson, as I live and breathe."

"That's the point, Viola. You are living and breathing," George said from the opposite side of the bed, where he and Lenny stood. Ernie slid in beside Aaron.

Viola turned her head, searching both sides of the bed. "You're here."

"Of course we're here for our best gal," Aaron said, his voice suddenly fierce. "Nothing could have kept us from you."

Viola's gaze lingered on Aaron for a moment. "But you already did what I asked you to do," she said, her eyes shining, her mouth pulled up in a smile that warmed the utilitarian room. "When I told you that both Connor and Ellie were heading for Las Vegas, I never expected you'd be able to bring them together so easily, let alone persuade them to get married."

"We didn't have to do anything," George laughed. "Tequila did the job for us."

Lenny frowned. "I think there was more to it than that. Those two had a past. And a past with someone you loved isn't always easy to forget."

Was Lenny talking about Connor and Ellie or the five of them? Aaron reached down and slipped his hand around Viola's arthritic fingers. The strength he never found in his own soul, he'd found in hers for years. Once again he was blanketed in the warmth of her unconditional love.

This time Viola was the vulnerable one. He could see the doubt and the worry that shadowed her eyes. It was time to give something back to the woman who'd been a good friend to all of them for so long. Aaron squeezed her fingers. "Our task is far from over. We might have helped Ellie and Connor get together. Now it's up to us to keep them that way."

Viola tried to sit up, but a racking cough sent her back against the mattress. "Yes," Viola rasped out when she was able, giving him a sad, gentle smile. In the next heartbeat, Viola stiffened. Her cardiac monitor beeped crazily up and down. She clamped on to Aaron's fingers, crushing them as she made a gasping sound.

"Push the 'Call' button. Go get help." Aaron signaled to the others as he stared at Viola, trying to remain calm for her sake. "I'm here with you, sugar. You're going to be fine." He could see the pain in her face.

"Please . . . don't let . . . me die."

"You won't die, Viola. Help is on the way. We still have so much to live for."

CHAPTER FOUR

Connor parked his everyday car, a gray Nissan LEAF, on the street in front of his grandmother's faded pink-and-white Victorian located on Capitol Hill. He made his way to the rock near the side of the house and retrieved the spare key his grandmother left for him there so that he would always have a place to call home. Yet Grayson House was no ordinary home.

The mansion drew from an Italianate style, laden with turrets, porches, bays embellished with gingerbread adornments, and fanciful windows. Victorians were like snowflakes; no two were alike, as proven by the ten houses in a row on this street.

With trepidation about what lay ahead, Connor made his way up the stairs to the front door. Ellie followed him. A thick manila envelope was perched against the wooden door. Picking it up, he noted the return address was the Seattle Historical Society.

He handed the packet to Ellie. "Looks like they really want Grayson House to be a part of their holiday showcase." Inserting the key in the lock, Connor stepped back for Ellie to enter.

With a heaviness that had nothing to do with Ellie, Connor followed her into his grandmother's house. The musty scent of a house in disrepair filled his senses. The old place would be filled with as much dust as memories—both of which he was in no hurry to confront. The thought had barely formed when Ellie stopped in front of a picture on the wall on the right side of the foyer. She reached out and touched the dusty frame, angling it to the same ninety degrees as the pictures on either side. "Isn't that your dad?" Ellie asked, obviously recognizing his father from when they'd dated in high school.

"And my mother," he replied. The photograph of his parents on their wedding day had retained its vibrant colors, looking out of place against the faded wallpaper behind it. His mother and father faced each other, holding hands, appearing as if they were in love. While his grandmother believed in true love and always lectured him about finding it, his own parents had shown him the truth. Love had limits. Lots of them.

"Oh," she replied, and dropped her fingers from the frame. He'd told her back in high school that his parents were no longer together. One year into his parents' marriage, Connor had been born. By their sixth anniversary, his mother was gone. Mary Grayson had walked out on his dad and him and had never come back. His father had never been the same after that. And, if Connor was honest, neither had he.

Ellie turned away, heading for the light switch. She flicked it on, and the chandelier overhead cast a yellow-brown light down on them. She surveyed the room. "Despite the dust and the cobwebs, this house really is a treasure."

The beautiful inlaid stonework beneath their feet was covered in dirt and dust, as was the grand staircase that rose before them, leading to the second story. Off to the left was a formal sitting room. On either side of the stairway were elegant plastered arches that framed the hallways beyond. "Are you happy you said yes to the project?" Connor asked.

"It will definitely be a challenge." She brought her gaze back to his.

"Have you ever supervised renovation work before?" Connor was suddenly curious about what she'd done during the past eleven years.

"No," she replied with a halfhearted smile. "But I'm very good at organizing work flow. I'll find contractors who can guarantee their work will be completed on time so we'll be done with the house by the time Viola recovers from her heart attack. Before you know it, we'll be free of each other."

That's what he wanted, wasn't it? Yet for some reason her words left him irritated. He turned away and moved into the parlor off to the right and flipped on the light. Beaten-gold luminescence revealed four walls once painted a dark red that were now faded to a brownish pink. The furnishings were two red and worn upholstered settees that faced each other, several small tables, bookshelves, and an intricately woven Turkish rug that covered the floor.

Ellie followed him inside the room and set the packet of papers down on a dusty side table near a settee. "Before we get settled, I'd like to set a few ground rules."

The huskiness in her voice washed over him, reminding him of a time, long ago, when she'd whispered sweet promises of a future together into his ear. Had she remembered those broken promises in Las Vegas? Had those memories bridged the divide time had created to bring them together again? He looked into her face. Eyes he'd always been able to read were closed off to him now. He took a slow step closer.

She didn't back away, but her breathing quickened. Her lips parted. "Are we agreed on that?"

He let his gaze drop to her lips. "On what?"

"That we should have rules." Her words were breathless.

"We don't need rules. What we need to be is convincing as a couple to my grandmother and to all our friends and family." The air between them all but crackled.

"What are you suggesting?" Her voice lowered even more, her tone provocative, challenging.

A muscle ticked in his jaw. "That we clear the air between us. It's obvious we both are harboring old resentment." The weight of their shared past hung in the air like the dust they'd stirred up upon entering the old house. They'd managed to hide from each other for eleven years. Was it long enough for them to put their unfinished business behind them? Or would they have it out, right here, right now?

"Given the choice, I would have picked anyone else to play the part of my wife, but destiny decided to bring us together instead," Connor said, trying unsuccessfully to keep the anger from his voice.

"Don't be so sanctimonious. We ended up in this position because of poor decisions on both of our parts. As a result, you now have a wife to present to your grandmother, and I have a much-needed job."

Connor drew a long, slow breath, trying desperately to pull himself out of the past. It was, as she pointed out, a win-win situation for them both. "Can you let go of our past in order for us to work together on this project while living in close proximity?"

Determination filled her eyes. "This house is huge. I doubt it would be hard to avoid each other."

"Then we have a truce?" he asked, extending his hand.

"Yes," she replied as she slipped her hand into his.

The palm of his hand warmed, tingling in a way it hadn't for years. He wasn't quite sure how they were going to pull the whole thing off— acting like a happily married couple, renovating the house, getting along when there was still so much between them, including an undeniable physical response to each other. Was it a spark from the past, or something else entirely?

◆ ◆ ◆

Ellie tried to focus on the present task despite the tingling sensation that passed between her and Connor's hands. They'd found a way to reconcile their past, however temporarily, as they worked toward a common goal. "I appreciate your grandmother's faith in my abilities to renovate and decorate this house."

"She wouldn't have offered if she didn't believe you could do everything she wanted."

Connor smiled, and Ellie realized it was the first real smile he'd given her since this whole Vegas wedding nightmare had begun. It softened the tiny lines at the corners of his eyes, making him look more like the boy she remembered. At the thought, butterflies let loose in Ellie's stomach.

"So where do we go from here?" she asked.

His green eyes grew serious again, and his smile vanished. His hands moved to her waist, and he slowly drew her against his chest. "Maybe we should get the awkwardness of this arrangement out of the way with a practice kiss. My grandmother will expect nothing less than a demonstration of our affection for each other."

"That sounds like a sound strategy," Ellie replied, trying to remind herself that this was all it was to Connor—a way to encourage his grandmother to get better.

Connor slowly pressed his lips against hers. Desire flared, bright and hot. The kind of desire she hadn't felt in years.

His lips firmed as he tilted his head. The kiss changed, and he was in command, parting her lips, invading her mouth, laying claim. Memories surged—brilliant moments she'd shared with this man when they'd both been idealistic and young. Need and desire infused her, and him, no longer a memory but real. Instead of fighting him, she tunneled her hands through his hair, surprising herself with her response as their mutual hunger launched them into a spiraling vortex. A small part of her brain reveled in the fact that she could still have this effect on him, that he could want her as much now as he had back then.

He pressed against her, his need as demanding as her own. Passion flared, hotter than she remembered. And suddenly she wanted more than just a kiss. They'd never gone beyond that in high school, but they were older and more experienced now.

And married.

Ellie tensed.

Connor's lips softened on hers, and he broke the kiss. He stared down into her eyes. "What's wrong?"

Her breath caught in her chest. "I can't believe I didn't ask this before. Do you have a girlfriend?"

"No," he replied, his voice still heavy with the passion they'd shared. "Do you have a boyfriend?"

She shook her head.

Satisfaction flared in his eyes. "That's good, because explaining our marriage would have been awkward otherwise."

She stepped back out of his reach. "Just how real do you expect this 'marriage' of ours to appear to our friends and family?"

"Are we back to those rules you talked about a few minutes ago?" he asked, still studying her lips.

She tried to look away but found she could not. "Do you expect me to share a bed with you?"

"While no one else is around, you can sleep wherever you want. But if we have guests, then we must maintain the illusion that we're sharing more than a house."

"Anything else?"

His gaze narrowed. "Are you talking about sex?"

She nodded again.

A smile pulled up the corners of his mouth. "Only if we both agree, but there will be no trying to fall in love."

"No worries there, Grayson. I learned that lesson long ago."

His smile vanished. "You know, maybe this whole situation happened for a reason. Maybe it's our chance to put our past behind us, and we can relearn how to be friends."

"Friends?" They had been friends once, before they'd let their attraction get out of hand. "For how long? Your grandmother could be around for years to come," she said, needing him to be specific about just how long this arrangement could continue.

"We can't know how long it will take Grandmother to heal, or to . . ." The words faded away as his voice became strained.

"Neither of us wants to be in this situation forever. Right?" Ellie asked.

He nodded. "I realize it's a lot to ask of you, to stay married to me for weeks on end. How about a compromise? We'll agree to stay married until Grayson House opens for the Holiday Street of Dreams."

"And if your grandmother isn't better by then?"

"The Holiday Street of Dreams is in five weeks. Grandmother should be recovered enough from her heart attack to handle the truth about our marriage."

Ellie studied the man before her. This wasn't the remote, distracted, and heartless Connor Grayson she remembered. The steady green eyes gazing back at her were warm and filled with genuine caring for his grandmother. A strange breathlessness came over her.

"Our arrangement won't be without its rewards, as that kiss just proved. We still have a chemistry that can be satisfying to us both."

There was no point in denying the truth of his words. They did have a spark that, if indulged properly, might be quite rewarding. If she were that kind of girl.

Which she wasn't.

She did believe in happily ever after despite what she'd told him in Vegas. So did her family. The Hawthornes prided themselves on never divorcing . . . ever. Marriage in her family was forever.

Ellie frowned. Maybe her family didn't have to know. It was only five weeks. If she were careful, she could keep the news of her marriage to Connor a secret. If her parents didn't know about her marriage, then there would be no repercussions, no disgrace. All she had to do was figure out a reason to miss Thanksgiving dinner.

She could walk away with a clear conscience, and maybe indulge herself in a little pleasure along the way. It would be a first for her to have a sexy, fun adventure. She was certain her girlfriends Jordan and Olivia would encourage her to be daring. "Can *you* be married to me for that long?" she asked.

"Of course," Connor said. "How hard can it be?"

She nodded, satisfied that they'd come to an agreement. "How hard, indeed."

Ellie had barely spoken the words when Connor's cell phone rang. He excused himself as he turned away from her, taking the call. It took less than a heartbeat to realize it wasn't a social call by the sudden stiffness of Connor's back.

"Dad, what's wrong?" Connor turned to face Ellie. Tension pulled his cheeks taut.

Silence hovered over the room until Connor spoke again. "Keep me posted on Grandmother's prognosis. Okay. Good night, Dad. Thanks for the update." Connor ended the call.

While Ellie waited, a million scenarios played across her mind. Had Viola taken a turn for the worse?

"My grandmother had a second heart attack," Connor replied, as though reading Ellie's thoughts.

"I'm so sorry." Ellie tried to be strong for him, but it was difficult to pull off. "Your grandmother is a fighter. She'll be okay—you'll see," she said, hoping that Viola's mind and spirit were hardy enough to defy the odds.

Connor stepped closer and touched Ellie's hand, so gently at first that she didn't realize what he'd done. "I can't lose her." His sadness was almost too much to bear. "I don't know what else to do."

Ellie saw his fear, his desperation, and although she didn't want to be moved by it, she couldn't resist. She reached up and touched his cheek. "It's okay to be afraid."

He turned into her touch and closed his eyes. "Viola was the only person who ever really understood me, far better than even my own father. She knew I wasn't like other kids and didn't try to change me. Viola accepted me for who I was."

He opened his eyes and looked at Ellie. "I've always known I would lose her someday, but I'm not ready."

Ellie smiled gently. "I wouldn't write Viola off just yet. She's not one to go quietly into the night. You gave her something to live for."

"We gave that to her," Connor corrected. "But will it be enough?"

"Only Viola can determine that." Ellie let her hand drop away from his cheek. "In the meantime, you know she's in good hands. I can call Jordan and ask her to check up on your grandmother if that will make you feel better."

He nodded, then stared at her for a long time as the fear in his eyes was replaced by resignation. "I don't know how to let her go. I've never been very good at good-bye."

With her next heartbeat, Ellie felt something that surprised her, a sudden comprehension about why their relationship had ended as it had, with him never showing up to the prom that night. Had he been too afraid to tell her good-bye as well?

For a second she remembered so much about the two of them, about what had drawn them together—his shyness, her loneliness, the vulnerability she'd seen in his eyes, the same vulnerability she shared. "There are no guarantees we'll get what we want out of life. But one thing is certain: you don't have to go through this alone." She reached for his hand this time, feeling a connection with this man that she hadn't felt in a very long time. "I'm not going anywhere."

"You said that to me once before," he said, his voice strained.

She flinched. "That was a long time ago, Connor."

He pulled away from her touch. "And sometimes it feels like yesterday. Anyway, I know it doesn't matter anymore, but I'm sorry we ended the way we did."

Ellie felt herself go hot, then cold. Of course it mattered. Their breakup had changed the course of her life.

Tense silence stretched between them as they stood there, seeing the old hurts in each other's eyes. Then his cell phone chimed. He reached for it. Glancing at the screen, he said, "It's my work. I need to take this," and left the room.

Ellie didn't move, just stood there as he walked away. She heard his voice through the fog of her mind as he answered the call. Pain twisted inside her. With only a few words he still had the power to hurt her, but she'd promised him she'd stay.

These would be the longest five weeks of her life.

CHAPTER FIVE

Ellie learned two important things about old houses on her first night at Grayson House: they were drafty, and they made lots of mysterious noises. After she and Connor had talked, they'd avoided each other for the rest of the night until finally they'd gone to bed in separate rooms.

Emotionally exhausted, Ellie had set up her space in the tower room above the master bedroom Connor had chosen. The room creaked and moaned as the October wind brushed past the old house. At first the sounds were unsettling, but soon she found them comforting as she lay on her bed, staring at the ceiling.

The stark reality of what she'd agreed to swam in her head. She had no doubts about fixing up the old house and decorating for the holiday open house. Both of those things were well within her abilities. But spending five weeks with a man who churned up so many memories might very well be her undoing.

She looked around her small room. The decorations were old but had a classic charm, much like the rest of the house. She could be comfortable here, especially since she'd gone back to her apartment after the hospital to gather enough clothes and personal items to get her through the next several weeks.

Ellie rolled off the bed and opened the bedside table, where she'd placed a picture of her and Connor from high school. Looking at the photograph now brought back all her old feelings of abandonment and betrayal, and not just from Connor. Years of broken promises by her father had started her on this path. She couldn't even count the number of times he'd promised to pick her up from school or take her somewhere, and then had never shown up because he was out fishing or engrossed in creating his newest lures. He'd buried his disappointment in not having a son in a passion that had consumed his every moment.

He'd broken her heart beyond repair at the junior high school father-daughter dance. Her father had promised he'd be there on time. Instead, he'd gone fishing with a friend. She'd waited by the door for an hour for him to show up. She knew he hadn't meant to be deliberately mean to her. He was her father, after all. He'd been as he always was—neglectful and never making her feel as though she were a priority.

Ellie stroked the photograph she held in her fingers as if by touching the image she could somehow transport herself back to that night. And, for the space of a single breath, she felt as if she were there. She remembered in that second the why and the how of her love for Connor. He'd been a geek to other people—but not to her. Whenever he looked at her, she always felt as if the warming rays of the sun were touching her skin. She closed her eyes and let that feeling wash over her again. A whole host of memories hit her at once: the sexy curve of his lips, the strength in his forearms when he crossed his arms over his chest, the deep rumble of his laughter.

She focused on the photograph once more. He'd made her heart thunder and her pulse quicken back then, especially when he'd said yes to her invitation to prom. Excitedly, they'd made plans—plans that went well beyond the dance. He would meet her in the gymnasium; then the two of them would head to Ellie's parents' cabin an hour away in the Cascade Range and spend their first night together.

Ellie had the evening all arranged. She'd gone to the cabin earlier that day and left a bottle of sparkling cider to chill, chocolates and strawberries to eat, and rose petals on the clean sheets, setting a romantic mood. There, they were going to plan their new life together, despite college, which would separate them temporarily.

Except that plan fell flat. Ellie had waited by the gym door for the first hour. The second hour, she sat outside, preferring not to see the other couples enjoying one another on what was supposed to be one of the biggest nights of their lives. As time stretched out before her, the old scars her father had inflicted became raw, mixing with this new, fresh wound.

And just when she thought her pain couldn't get much worse, Connor had sent Mrs. Phillips, the physics teacher, to find her, with a note saying he'd been detained by the recruiters. Mrs. Phillips looked at her with pitying eyes. She had rattled off several excuses for Connor's absence and how important the interviews were to his future. In some part of her brain, Ellie understood. But she wondered, with equal parts pain and sorrow, why she was never a priority for the men in her life. Connor knew how important that night was to her, to them. With tears in her eyes, Ellie had sent a note back to Connor:

Tonight was a mistake. I wish you the best of luck.

Fresh tears fell from her eyes. She squeezed her eyes shut, battling the painful memories with everything inside her. Now they were married. And she felt just as abandoned as ever.

Suddenly she was both emotionally and physically exhausted by the reality of her future—a temporary future—with a man who still sent her pulse quivering. Perhaps it was better to remember the heartache than to long for something more from Connor Grayson. With a sigh, she put the photo back in the drawer. If she needed motivation to stay detached, she knew where to find it.

◆ ◆ ◆

The next morning, Ellie—dressed in jeans, a navy-blue T-shirt, and a soft yellow cardigan—made her way down two sets of stairs to the ground floor. Even though an ache still lingered in her heart, she decided to stop dwelling on the past and start looking to the future. Viola had given her a great gift in Grayson House, and she would do everything in her power to make the project a success.

The goal for the day, apart from contacting contractors, was to clear the house of dust, cobwebs, and dirt to see what they'd truly be working with. She shivered at the thought of all the spiders lurking in the shadows.

Back in the kitchen, Ellie discovered a closet filled with cleaning supplies and a vacuum. She smiled. There would be a long hose between her and those spiders as soon as they revealed themselves.

She had barely finished the thought when Connor entered the kitchen dressed in khaki pants and a dress shirt. "Did you sleep well?" he asked, with a truly concerned look on his face.

"Better than I expected." Ellie retrieved a mop and bucket, then shut the closet door. She frowned as she got a good look at Connor. "You're a little overdressed for cleaning the house."

"I can't today. I'm off to work," he replied, snatching an apple she'd brought from her apartment off the table.

Ellie moved closer. "You're my co-foreman on this job."

"Not today," he replied.

"Does that mean you're willing to defer all decisions about this project to me, because that's the only way we will finish this job in five weeks?"

Connor frowned. "I'll be gone for one day—"

"That's your excuse today. And tomorrow?"

He took a bite of the apple, then glanced at her, puzzled. "I'm caught between this house and my job. What else can I do?"

"Help me clean," she said, keeping her tone even.

He paused, taking another bite. "I will help. But I need to do my part in the evenings after work. I have a robotic car to finish, Ellie."

"Don't do this." Her control slipped as her temper built. It was happening again. The men in her life always had other priorities besides her.

His face set. "Do what?"

"We're both supposed to refurbish this house, but if you have better things to do, then do them. This house renovation is a huge break for my career. I'm taking this opportunity and maximizing it, with or without your help."

A myriad of emotions played across his face—anger, confusion, then finally acceptance. "I appreciate that you're here, helping my grandmother . . . and me. I know you're more than capable of taking the lead on this project. I have no choice but to go into the lab at the university today. I've had no time to reorganize my staff and figure out how I can do more oversight than the actual development on the car. But I'll try to be here tomorrow."

"I do understand about having no time to arrange things. Both of our lives are different since Las Vegas. Go into the office, and I'll see you tonight." Without waiting for a response, she turned away and strode down the hallway. A moment later she heard the front door close.

Alone once more, Ellie looked around her. It was her first day in this humongous house. She had no doubts about her ability to get this job done on schedule and under budget. It was time to convince everyone else. With that thought, Ellie picked up the mop and bucket. It was still a few hours before she could call any of the contractors. She might as well get started on the cleaning. She'd start at the front of the house and work her way back. She might not be able to control much of the situation she currently found herself in, but she could at least conquer how much dust they tracked from room to room.

◆ ◆ ◆

By two o'clock, Ellie not only had a plan for the renovation but she'd wrestled the first floor of the house into livable shape. The surfaces were clean, the spiders and cobwebs were gone, and all the lightbulbs that were burned out had been replaced with energy-efficient LEDs.

Once she could sit on a clean chair and not freak out about the spiders nearby, she'd contacted several contractors, who'd agreed to come out tomorrow and give her bids on the projects she'd identified as priorities—the roof leaked, a section of the siding on the western side of the house had dry rot, a window on the second story at the back of the house was broken, and just about every surface, inside and out, needed fresh paint.

She knew from past wedding projects she'd taken on in older venues that the repairs were essential before any decorating could take place. Once she had a canvas that was sturdy and safe, then she could add the paint, creating a masterpiece. At least that was the way she looked at the Grayson House project. The fundamentals of a good roof, walls, and windows were first, then paint and furnishings, followed by the part she enjoyed the most—creating a look and feel that was as unique as it was inspiring.

With a final glance around her at the work she'd done, Ellie was about to take a lunch break when someone knocked at the door. She wasn't expecting any of the contractors until tomorrow, so who could it be?

As soon as she opened the door, she got her answer. A thick vellum business card was thrust at her, bearing a name and, below that, "attorney-at-law." "Georgia Burke to see Connor and Ellie Grayson."

Ellie took the card, then stiffened at the lawyer's words. *Grayson.* She was a Grayson. It was the first time she'd actually considered that fact. Her fingers started to shake, and she wished desperately she still held the mop, as she had all morning. It would give her something solid to hold on to. Something to focus on other than the lawyer's confused eyes.

It's only temporary.

Ellie seized the comforting thought until her fingers stopped shaking and the lump in her throat melted away. She drew a breath and asked, "Did Connor send you?"

"Heavens, no," Georgia said with a frown. "I represent Viola Grayson. She sent me. I have papers for both you and Connor to sign."

"Viola isn't well. How could she have sent you?" Ellie objected.

The lawyer raised a brow. "My client was able to communicate her needs. Now, may I come in?" she asked stiffly.

Ellie stepped back and waved the tall, no-nonsense woman inside. "Connor's not here, but you're welcome to come in and talk with me."

The lawyer reached for a brown travel bag near her feet that Ellie hadn't noticed before. She strode into the house and set the bag down in the foyer. "Where is Connor?" Georgia's frown made it clear she wasn't pleased. "He's supposed to be here. That was Viola's agreement with the two of you."

"He had to go into work and arrange things with his staff. He'll be back soon." Ellie had no idea when Connor would return, but she wasn't about to let the lawyer know that. And because she knew this wasn't a social call, Ellie asked bluntly, "Why are you here?"

An odd half smile tugged at the corners of Georgia's lips as she bent down and unzipped the bag. A gray-and-white-striped tabby jumped out.

The cat stared up at Ellie with lazy interest. "You brought a cat?"

"He used to live here with Viola but has been with a foster pet family since Viola moved into the assisted-living facility. Since the house is now occupied, Viola wanted him returned. He's your cat now."

She didn't know anything about cats. "But—"

"The papers Viola sent over outline everything she expects of you and Connor while you live in and refurbish Grayson House. Zanzibar is simply another one of your new obligations."

Ellie looked down at her new pet. Two gold eyes watched her with suspicion. *Zanzibar.* Who named a cat something like that? "What does he eat?"

Georgia set the bag of cat food on the now perfectly polished mosaic floor. "There are directions on the back. Now." She bent and retrieved a leather binder from the outside pocket of the bag. "Let's get down to business. There are several papers I need to go over with you, including a certificate of approval I received from the Historic Preservation Board."

A half hour later, Ellie had signed several legal documents. She had to give Viola credit for being thorough. The older woman had had her lawyer draw up a contract for the renovation budget, her remodeling expectations, and even a cohabitation agreement for Ellie, Connor, and the cat. And Viola had already vetted any legal issues they might have with the city of Seattle for the renovations to the house.

Quiet acceptance settled inside Ellie. She not only had her first paycheck; she and Connor had a bank account with enough money to see to the restoration as well as living expenses for the next several weeks.

Connor would have his own papers to sign, but Viola had come through on her promise to fund his research. And for her grandson, she'd also included a power of attorney and a last will and testament.

"Viola's preparing for her death," Georgia said slowly, her hawkish brown eyes watching Ellie.

For a moment, everything went quiet and still as fear crept along Ellie's spine. Connor had told her he wasn't ready to lose his grandmother, but even their pretending to be in love might not be enough to change that fate. All Ellie could do was play along, pretending to be worthy of what Viola had just given her—a way to move forward with her business, a livelihood, and a cat.

Unable to maintain eye contact with the lawyer, Ellie dropped her gaze to the cat, who didn't look extremely pleased with this new living arrangement.

"Viola loves that cat. She wouldn't hand him over to just anyone," Georgia said. "You should count yourself lucky."

"I do," Ellie said, then groaned inwardly. Those were the words that had put her in this position in the first place.

To Ellie's surprise, the lawyer smiled. "Good. I'll see myself out. Let Connor know I need his signature."

Before Ellie could respond, Georgia picked up her brown bag and disappeared through the door, leaving her alone with the cat. In the sudden silence, Ellie bent down. "Welcome to Grayson House." She reached out, her palm cupped and low, toward the animal in a gesture of friendship.

The cat shifted away from her.

Not friends yet.

Ellie straightened. "Okay, have it your way." She picked up the cat food, taking it with her to the kitchen. "Maybe a little lunch might soften your mood." Over her shoulder, she could see Zanzibar reluctantly following.

CHAPTER SIX

At five o'clock, Ellie stopped work for the day. After she'd showered and changed into a comfortable pair of leggings, a long cream-colored sweater, and her favorite brown boots, she headed for the kitchen.

On the table was a bouquet of yellow-and-orange flowers that hadn't been there before, with a handwritten note that read:

Meeting you again was the best thing that's happened to me all year. —C

She looked around the kitchen. Had Connor come home? Ellie moved to the back door and tried the knob. It remained locked, so she opened the door and looked outside as though expecting to see Connor waiting there. With a shake of her head, she moved back inside and closed the door, leaving it unlocked. She listened to the silence. There was no one home besides her, yet somehow flowers had magically appeared. Maybe Connor had come home during the day and had left them for her as a surprise?

A thrill moved through her that she couldn't hold back at his thoughtful gesture. Grinning, she returned to the kitchen and made herself a cup of tea.

Sitting at the table, she admired her cleaning work, trying not to think about the fact she would have to do the very same cleaning to the second and third floors tomorrow.

Right now every surface before her glistened, even if the ugly wallpaper curled halfway down the wall, and the paint was faded and dull in each and every room. At her feet sat the cat. Zanzibar still hadn't deigned to let her touch him, but he hadn't left her side since arriving at the house.

They'd be friends from a distance.

The back door flew open, and Ellie whipped around to see Connor stride into the house. His presence filled the kitchen, and she suddenly realized how empty the home had been while he was gone. She'd been alone before Connor had come into her life. So why was she suddenly looking for company?

"How'd you know I'd be in the kitchen?" she asked, setting her cup down on the table.

"I didn't." He stepped inside and shut the door against the wind. "The front door was locked, and I forgot to bring the key with me. The doorbell is obviously broken. When I knocked, no one answered, so I thought I'd try the kitchen door." He didn't remove his coat. "You've been busy," he said, looking around the kitchen. "Did you clean the whole house?"

"Just the first floor."

He frowned. "Why didn't you wait for a cleaning crew?"

She shrugged. "I'm used to being busy. I needed something to take my mind off—"

"Me?" Suddenly all his focus was on her.

"Believe it or not, I have lots of things to think about that don't involve you, Grayson."

"Darn," he replied. "Because I thought about you all day."

She was startled by his admission. "Am I supposed to be charmed?"

"I suppose that was too much to hope for." His rueful laugh filled the kitchen as he set his messenger bag on the table. From the front pocket, a piece of sheet music slid out.

Ellie picked it up. "What's this?"

He plucked it from her grasp before she could get a good look at the title. "You should know." He gave her a smile that was both sexy and shy.

She frowned, not understanding.

His gaze dropped to her feet. "When did we get a cat?"

"Your grandmother's lawyer brought him by."

Connor bent down and ruffled the cat's fur. "Now I recognize you. Hello, Zanzibar."

Ellie didn't know whether to be offended that *he* could pet the cat, or grateful someone could.

"Get your coat. I want to show you something." He stood. His gaze moved from her hair to her breasts, which were barely outlined beneath her thick sweater, to her hips. There was something warm and inviting in his look.

Heat flooded Ellie's cheeks as she stood. Hiding her face from further inspection, she hurried down the hallway to retrieve her coat. The entire way, she could feel Connor's gaze on her back. She opened the front closet and retrieved one of the coats she'd moved there earlier today. "Where are we going?"

He offered her his arm. "I wanted to take you for a ride in the prototype of my self-driving car."

She took his arm and walked with him out the front door. After locking the door, she allowed him to lead her down the front stairs. "They let you take the car home?"

"It's my car. So far all the funding has been mine, until Viola stepped up. Then today another amazing thing happened." He stopped before the small white car and opened the door.

"What happened?" she asked as she slipped into the passenger side, slightly uncomfortable that there was no steering wheel or any other visible electronics that would give the occupant control over the car.

He joined her on what would have been the driver's side. "The CEO of Microtech came to the lab today. He congratulated us on our marriage."

"How did he know we were married? Nobody in Washington knows but your father, Viola, and Jordan."

Connor twisted toward her. "He said he read about it in the *Seattle Gazette*."

Ellie's heart dropped to her toes. *How did that happen so quickly?* They'd been married for only two days. "Somebody leaked the news to the press?" Did her parents see it? Oh heavens, she'd catch so much guff from them.

"Looks like they did," he replied with a pleased smile. "Whoever it was had to have high-level connections in order to get the announcement in so quickly."

"I don't know anyone with connections like that. Do you?"

"No."

Ellie brought her fingers to her temples, trying to hold back the headache that threatened. "What did the CEO want?"

Connor's eyes brightened. "He said he likes to work with family men. Not only did he offer me financial support, but he also wants to partner with my University of Washington development team, using his company's proprietary software for the onboard computer. With Microtech's support, we'll be further into development than any of the other designs out there. If we're first to market, it will mean billions in sales. And I hold the majority of the patents."

"I'm really happy that everything you've worked so hard for is paying off. What an incredible feat to build the first successful self-driving car." The words were sincere, yet at the moment fear blinded her to all else. Her parents would be upset to learn about her marriage in the newspaper. And when she told them she would be divorced soon, they would be disappointed in her—again. She'd been living under a veil of disappointment for so long, she wondered why she even tried to please them anymore. They'd wanted a son. They'd even had a name picked out: Edward. How many times had she heard the tales? They'd planned to have a second child, but her mother's pregnancies never held after Ellie was born. After five miscarriages, her parents had finally given up. And they'd resigned themselves to having only a daughter.

Even though she knew they wouldn't be pleased that she'd disappointed them once again, she had to see them to explain. "How do you drive this thing?"

"You don't." He gave her a cocky smile. "It's a self-driving car."

She sighed, her irritation growing. "How do you make it go where you want?"

He pointed to a speaker on the dashboard. "You talk to the onboard computer. Where do you want to go?"

She gave him the address but didn't tell him exactly where they were headed. Maybe he'd remember her old address from so long ago. He'd met her parents before. Initially they'd liked him, until he'd broken their only daughter's heart.

The car started forward, merging with traffic. A shiver of apprehension worked its way across her neck. How strange to let a machine have total control over your safety. Although, as they moved down Aloha Avenue, she was almost certain she could walk faster than the car was driving. "Why is it going so slow?"

"We're working on accuracy, not speed at the moment," he explained. "I've received a few tickets in this prototype for driving too slow."

"I can believe that." Thank goodness her parents didn't live too far away or it might take hours to get to their destination. A lifetime later, they arrived at the address Ellie had given Connor. The car parallel-parked on the street across from Volunteer Park's north side and in front of her parents' house.

"Are we going to the park?" Connor asked as his brows knit in confusion.

"No," she said, opening the car door and getting out. "You're meeting my parents. Again."

His face paled. "You could have warned me."

"And let you talk your way out of it? Not a chance." She grabbed his hand and almost pulled him up the driveway. Porch lights illuminated their way, revealing a crisply cut lawn and tidy flower beds. Fall color dappled the leaves on the trees while rambling rosebushes offered late blooms and a sweet scent to the early evening air.

They made their way up the stairway to the redbrick house. The house had been built in the 1920s in the Tudor style. Her parents had purchased the home thirty years ago. They'd remodeled once, updating the electrical and plumbing, and expanded the kitchen and family room at the back of the house.

Instead of walking in, as she would have usually done, she rang the doorbell. It seemed as if she should, given that she was bringing not just her boyfriend but her *husband* to the house.

"In all the time we were together our senior year, you only brought me over here a few times. Will your parents even remember me?" She could hear the fear in his voice.

"I doubt you have anything to worry about. They will be so focused on me and how much I've disappointed them by not telling them about our marriage that they'll probably not even notice you."

"What are your parents doing now?" Connor asked with a hint of anxiousness as they waited.

"Dad is still an engineer, building planes. Mom changed jobs a few years ago and now works as an accountant with a firm downtown." They were not wealthy by any means, but they were comfortable.

"Why will your parents be disappointed?" Connor asked as they heard footsteps approaching the door.

"I've never felt like I was enough," Ellie said, leaving her explanation at that. Connor would learn the truth soon enough.

The door opened, revealing her mother. Julie Hawthorne looked at the two of them in surprise at first; then her sharp, hazel-brown eyes shifted from Ellie to Connor and back again. "Ellie, sweetie, so good to see you." Her mother came forward to greet her with a kiss on the cheek. "And Connor Grayson." She turned to him. "You've definitely changed for the better over the years."

"Mom," Ellie groaned.

Her mother relaxed. "I must say this is a surprise, even though we already read about your marriage in this morning's newspaper."

Ellie felt the blood rush from her face. They were too late. "I can explain."

"Why didn't you tell us?" her mother asked, stepping aside for the two of them to enter. Surprisingly, there was no judgment in her voice.

"It happened so quickly—"

"Not the marriage, dear. Why didn't you tell us you were dating Connor?"

Ellie was momentarily taken aback; her mother seemed less disturbed about the marriage than the details of her dating life.

Connor stepped forward and took Julie's hands in his. "We didn't want to get anyone's hopes up in case things didn't work out between us again," he said with his most charming smile. "My grandmother felt the same way—a little surprised but ultimately happy Ellie and I found each other again after all these years."

Her mother blushed. "Ellie always said you were a charmer."

"Mother!" Ellie groaned again. She didn't need to tell him that detail from the past.

"Don't 'Mother' me. It's true, and you know it." Her mother hooked her arm through Connor's and led him farther into the house, toward the family room, where they would no doubt find her dad. "James, look who stopped by," she called as they walked.

Ellie followed along. At least her mother wasn't angry with her about their secret wedding. Instead, she seemed enchanted by her charming son-in-law. He was charming when he wanted to be, Ellie conceded, but her parents also knew he was the boy who'd broken her heart.

They entered the family room, and her father was just where she suspected he'd be—sitting at his hobby table, tying flies along a mechanical arm for his next fishing trip. He stopped and regarded Connor with a great deal of interest.

"Dad, do you remember Connor Grayson?"

He left his hobby table to come around and shake Connor's hand. "Nice to see you again, son. It's been a long time."

"That was entirely my fault, I'm afraid," Connor said without looking at Ellie. "You know teenage boys. They get their priorities all wrong."

Her father's laugh grated over her as she stood frozen, unable to dredge up a coherent thought. Had Connor just apologized for abandoning her? Or was he making excuses? If only he would look at her. And then he did.

In his eyes she saw the truth. He was sorry for leaving her alone.

Pain snagged her heart and tears stung her eyes, but she forced them back, refusing to let her emotions get the best of her in front of him, in front of her parents. She focused on her mother, who scooped up the morning's newspaper from the coffee table. It was open to the announcements page. She'd circled the news about Ellie and Connor in red pen.

"Oh, Ellie. This is the best news we've had in a long time." Her mother thrust the paper into Ellie's hands. "We couldn't be happier."

Ellie clutched the paper, scanning the announcement. Her parents' reaction wasn't what she'd imagined at all. "I don't understand. I thought you'd be angry I got married without telling you, without you even being there."

Her dad patted her arm. "Sweetheart, don't take this the wrong way, but ever since you started that event-planning business of yours, where you've planned such extravagant weddings for others, I've lived in terror of how your mother and I would ever afford any wedding you wanted to have. You did want something on a grand scale, right?"

He didn't wait for her answer as he plowed right on. "By getting married in Las Vegas, you just saved us thousands of dollars. We were so excited to read your announcement in this morning's paper that we booked a cruise with the money we'd saved. We're finally going to one of the places on our bucket list."

On wooden legs, Ellie moved to the couch to sink into the plush cushions. She took a deep breath, then another, with an exaggerated calm she didn't feel. What was happening? Who had swapped her parents with aliens?

The realization hit as she watched her dad not only lead Connor over to his hobby table but sit him down in front of his latest creation and encourage him to try his hand at tying a fly. Her father now had the son he'd always wanted.

"I'm calling this one a pinkie," James said. "It's a combination of bucktail and pink ostrich feathers. The fish will love it." Her dad bent over and showed his new son-in-law how to wrap the ostrich feathers around the hook shank. "Do you fish, son?"

"No," Connor replied with a laugh. "I've been in laboratories most of my life. There are no rivers or lakes there."

James clapped Connor on the back in a friendly, fatherly way. "Well, you'll have to go fishing with me this coming weekend. The season is winding down. Clear your schedule for Sunday. I'll pick you up at four a.m. We'll try this little baby out."

"That early?"

Her dad studied Connor with increasing contentment. "That's when the fish are biting, son."

Ellie scowled. Her parents knew her history with Connor, yet none of that seemed to matter. In fact, having her parents like Connor so intensely would only make their eventual divorce that much worse. They would blame her for the failure, for not giving the marriage her all.

Coming here was a big mistake.

"Ellie," her mother said, coming to stand before her, "do you have a minute for a walk in the garden?"

This was the mother she was more used to—the one who would speak to her in private about her mistakes. Even though she'd expected such a response, Ellie's stomach fluttered with nerves as she stood and followed her from the room.

Her mom stopped beside a back doorway and handed Ellie one of her old sweaters that still hung on a rack. "You'll need this."

"Thanks, Mom." Slipping the sweater over her shoulders, Ellie followed her mother out into the cool evening air. Shades of pink and lavender and blue blurred the edges of the day as it turned into night.

They walked in companionable silence as they made their way across the huge expanse of green grass that made up the backyard. With every step, Ellie's nerves coiled tighter and tighter. What did her mom want to talk about that they had to discuss alone?

"I hope your dad didn't hurt your feelings with the comment about the cruise," her mom finally said. "We're both just so happy for you to finally have found someone."

Ellie sighed. "I'm not trying to be alone, Mom. I just haven't found anyone . . ."

At her mother's quizzical look, she amended, "Until Connor."

Her mom stopped walking. "I'm happy to hear that. Almost as happy as I am to learn about the baby."

"The baby?" Ellie felt as if she were suddenly falling and there was no one there to catch her.

"Well, of course. Why else would you go to Las Vegas and come home married?"

Feeling off balance, Ellie drew a shaky breath. "I'm not pregnant." At least she hoped she wasn't. She didn't even know if they'd had sex! "We've only been married a few days. Why on earth would you think I was pregnant?"

Her mom's eyes twinkled. "A mom knows these things."

A nervous laugh filled the space between them. "In this case you're wrong, so very, very wrong."

She took Ellie's hands and suddenly regarded her with a slightly suspicious air. "Is everything okay?"

Ellie forced a smile to her lips. Part of her wanted to confess right then and there that her marriage to Connor wasn't real before her parents became too invested in finally having the son they'd always wanted, but she forced that desire down deep inside. "Everything's fine, Mom. It couldn't be better."

Fine.

One word that held infinite meanings.

◆ ◆ ◆

Connor watched as Ellie and her mother strolled past the back windows while he and her father finished tying the pink fly they would use this weekend on their fly-fishing adventure. James continued to talk about where they would go and what they would do. All Connor could think about was the pained look in Ellie's eyes when her parents had welcomed him without hesitation. In the past two days he'd figured out why Ellie had reacted so badly to his missing the prom. It wasn't that he hadn't shown up. It was that he'd been one more person to set her feelings aside and treat her as if she weren't important. He'd known about her issues with her family back then, yet he'd done exactly the same thing to her.

And today, when tears threatened to push past her facade of strength, he'd almost dropped to his knees. In that moment, he knew he had to do something to equalize the situation—to give her a long-overdue apology.

Suddenly James stopped talking. "Do you love her?" he asked, following the path of Connor's gaze.

Love her? I did once. Do I love her still? Connor frowned. "How can you ask that?" he replied, avoiding the question. Her dad's eyes were watchful, perhaps too watchful, as Connor shifted his gaze to the floor. "I married your daughter and intend to honor that commitment as long as she'll have me." The words were true enough, and they must have satisfied James because he thumped Connor on the back in a gesture of bonding.

"Be good to my little girl. Besides her mother, she's all I have."

"I will," Connor replied with sincerity. "Ellie's a special person. She always has been."

James nodded. "I'm glad you recognize that." He pushed away from the hobby table. "Follow me. Julie and I have a wedding present for the two of you. It's a Hawthorne family tradition."

Connor followed him down the hallway to the living room, uncertain what to expect.

The older man stopped before a grandfather clock. "This clock has been in our family for six generations. It came to this country with my ancestors from England. It's been handed down from Hawthorne male to Hawthorne male." He shrugged. "Since I have no sons, it goes to Ellie . . . and to you."

They'd only been married for two days, and they were already getting bogged down in family traditions and lies. When he'd asked Ellie to stay married to him for Viola's sake, he hadn't considered all the people who might be hurt in the aftermath of their charade.

"Thank you for this very generous gift, James. How about we leave the clock right here until Ellie and I are more settled?"

"Not a chance," he protested. "Not only is this clock a tradition—it's good luck to the marriage of those who own it. There's never been a divorce in our family for the past six generations or more. This clock is the reason why. You must take it with you right now."

"I doubt it will fit in my car," Connor said, cringing at the man's words. James might like him now, but the man would hate him when all this was over. The darn clock and its good luck would be broken. All because of him.

CHAPTER SEVEN

The next morning, Ellie frowned at the grandfather clock Connor and her father had deposited in the foyer of Grayson House last night. She'd always hated the heirloom.

"Too bad our family tradition ends here with you, daughter." Her father had sighed with regret many times in front of the clock.

At first she'd tried to persuade her father that since they were of English descent, and because England could recognize a female queen, he should accept a female heir.

That argument had gone nowhere, and over the years, she was reduced to simply rolling her eyes and proclaiming that both she and the clock were innocents in all this. That was until one day when she looked closely at the face of the clock and saw not an ordinary clock face, but the face of an old man.

No wonder the Hawthorne males loved the clock so much. He was one of them.

Old Man Hawthorne stared at her now as he had the residents of whatever house he'd occupied over the centuries, judging them, warning them not to make a false step in any Hawthorne marriage. The steady ticking of the old clock could easily be accompanied by a wagging finger of warning.

Ellie narrowed her gaze, trying to warn the old man in return. "You don't belong here in this house, especially if you're going to see too much. So keep that frown to yourself or you'll find yourself on the front lawn. Got it?"

The old man continued to frown.

Ellie groaned. "Okay, fine. I can't move you by myself, but you don't have to watch us." With a sudden, satisfied grin, she cast an old sheet up and over the crown, covering the clock. If her parents asked her why she'd covered their wedding gift, she'd simply explain she was keeping the antique safe from all the construction at the house.

The day passed quickly as she and Connor worked side by side, cleaning the upper floors and meeting with contractors. The bids for the roof, new siding and windows, and painting would come in tomorrow. Until then, they had plenty to do themselves. With the rest of her day, Ellie set about stripping the foyer of its old wallpaper.

Methodically she mixed up then spread the remover solvent across the aging paper. By the time she made her way around the front room, it was time to start peeling the paper off. Scraper in hand, she started at the top. Since most of the decorative covering had started falling off on its own, it took little effort to convince the rest to follow.

The most difficult part was moving the double ladder along the wall. Trying to save time, instead of getting down and moving the ladder, Ellie leaned out, struggling to reach the next row of paper.

Too late she recognized her mistake when the ladder wobbled and pitched away from her. With nothing to support her, she reached out and grabbed the only thing she could, the cloth covering the clock. The sheet slithered to the floor, doing nothing to break her fall. She fell . . . right into Connor's arms.

Ellie shrieked at the unexpected rescue. Strength wrapped around her. "I'm so sorry."

"Don't be sorry." He held her close to his chest. "It's not every day I get to rescue a damsel in distress."

Heat flooded her cheeks. "I wasn't distressed, just stupid." While she might not like the idea of being rescued, she did appreciate the way his arms cradled her as though she was precious and worth saving.

Time seemed to stand still as they stared into each other's eyes. There was something different in his expression—something she couldn't name. Warmth flamed inside her.

"I've got to go," Ellie said, breaking the moment.

"Can I ask you something?" Connor asked at the same time. He lowered her to the ground. When she was stable on her feet, he released her. "Where are you going?"

"You wanted to ask me something?" Again they spoke at the same time.

He reached for her, settled his hands on her waist, and simply held her. "We've gone about this whole thing wrong. We might be legally married, but we skipped every step in a relationship to get there."

"What are you saying?" Ellie asked, not sure if she was frightened or excited at where this conversation might lead.

"It's what I'm asking you," he clarified. "Let me make amends for my misdeeds in the past. Will you go on a date with me tomorrow night?"

She startled. Although it had been obvious he was interested in her, it had taken Connor five months to ask her out when they were in high school. Things were definitely improving with their timing. "You're ready to put the past behind us?"

"It's time, don't you think?"

She nodded.

"Good. It's a date then. Leave everything to me." He bent and pressed a kiss to her forehead, then released her. "Where did you say you were headed?"

"My friends Jordan, Olivia, and I meet every Tuesday night. It's kind of a tradition."

His eyes narrowed. "You and yours have lots of traditions."

Her gaze strayed to the clock. She turned her back on the face of the old man still frowning there. "Some are better than others."

"Have fun. I'm going to head into my lab on the university campus while you're gone. We're finalizing the final stages of the new computer system. I don't want to leave the engineering to anyone else," he said, leaving her alone in the foyer with the grandfather clock.

Ellie glanced up at the timepiece once more, and her breath caught. Was it her imagination, or did the corner of the old man's mouth bend up in a smile?

◆ ◆ ◆

Ellie stood outside The Lucky Club forty minutes later. Fat, cold drops of rain fell from the sky as wind swirled around her feet. Without an umbrella to shield her, water slithered down her face and onto her neck, but she wasn't ready to go inside yet.

Jordan would have told Olivia that she was married. The fingers of her right hand moved over to her left, twisting the diamond ring Connor had given her around and around. She'd attempted to take the ring off before coming tonight, but she found she didn't have the will to slip it off her finger. It was important to her to honor the agreement she and Connor had made.

Dropping her hands to her sides, she pushed forward through the arched doorway and into the noisy bar. Her friends would expect to hear all about her trip to Las Vegas and the strange turn her life had taken there. She drew in a fortifying breath and moved toward their usual table in the back.

Olivia and Jordan were already there. Olivia waved to her, spotting her the moment she entered the room. Olivia looked so much more at ease since she and Max had married. Instead of her brunette hair coiled up at the back of her head, she'd left her wavy locks free to fall across her shoulders and down her back. "Hey, you," Olivia greeted her with a smile.

Ellie slid into a chair opposite her two friends. "What a weekend," she said.

"I'm dying to hear how the two of you hooked up," Jordan said, taking a sip of her champagne.

"Congratulations." Olivia's dark eyes glittered with happiness. "Jordan told me your news. We're having an impromptu bridal shower tonight. We brought you presents." Two packages were stacked in the center of the table, wrapped in silver-and-gold paper.

Ellie frowned. "Presents for me?"

"Of course," Olivia said. "It's not every day one of our friends gets married."

Ellie fingered her wedding ring again, suddenly unsure about boasting to her friends that she was only in this thing for the short haul, not forever.

"Forget the presents," Jordan said, pushing a waiting glass of pink champagne Ellie's way. With her pale skin, short black hair, and green eyes, Jordan's Irish heritage was undeniable. Her fiery temper was just as fierce. "Why on earth did you marry Connor Grayson? Tell us every detail."

Ellie reached for her champagne and took a long drink in an effort to ease a sudden tightness in her throat. She set the drink down, and still she hesitated.

These two women were her best friends. In the past, they'd told one another everything. It wasn't that she didn't trust them with the truth now. It was that she didn't trust her own response when she told them. She struggled not to close her eyes and let herself remember the feeling of being in Connor's arms. She'd forgotten how gentle he was—forgotten how he could make her feel protected and breathless at the same moment.

She drew a tight breath and forced the memory away. "We met in Las Vegas. The details are a little fuzzy."

Olivia frowned. "What would make the memory fuzzy?"

"You were drunk, weren't you?" Jordan sat back in her chair with a measuring smile.

"A little." Ellie admitted the partial truth with a wince.

"Ha!" Jordan exclaimed.

"Ignore Jordan. I'm sure it was magical," Olivia replied with a warning glance at Jordan. "How could your wedding be anything but an event?"

Pressing her lips together, Ellie dug into her purse and pulled out the one picture she'd kept from those the Elvises had brought to their room the morning after. She held it out to Olivia and Jordan. "Not that I remember much, but this proves it wasn't exactly the wedding I'd always dreamed of."

A crack of laughter escaped Jordan. "You got married by Elvis?"

Ellie nodded. "In the Chapel of Burning Love with three other Elvis impersonators as our attendants."

"For you, the wedding planner, to be married by Elvis impersonators." Jordan snorted. "That's hysterical."

"I'm an event planner," Ellie corrected. Why did everyone always get that wrong?

Olivia frowned, studying the picture. She looked off into the distance, then returned her gaze to Ellie. "How many Elvises were there?"

"Four. Why?"

Oliva set the picture on the table in front of Ellie. "It's nothing. I'm probably imagining things that aren't there."

Ellie's frown deepened as she turned in the direction Olivia had indicated. Four men sat at a table across the room, their heads buried in the newspaper. From what she could see, they looked nothing like the men they'd met in Las Vegas . . . but, then again, they'd been in costume.

Still, the chances of the same four men being in Seattle were slim to none. Ellie turned back to her friends with a sigh. "It's been the weirdest week of my life. I'm married and living in and working on Connor's grandmother's house. It's my first-ever design job."

Olivia's brows came together. "His grandmother hired you?"

She nodded. "Plus, I'll be able to fund my Birthday Project through June of next year. I can't wait for you both to see Grayson House. It has so much potential and deserves to be restored to its old glory. Every time I walk through a room, I see so many possibilities."

"That's terrific, Ellie. Sounds like you really love the old place. What will you be doing?" Olivia asked.

"I've broken the job down into three stages. The first stage will be renovations to the exterior of the house. The second will be remodeling the interior. And, finally, the part I love, staging the event decorations."

"What event?" Jordan asked.

"The Holiday Street of Dreams at the end of November."

"Oh, Ellie," Olivia said. "What a great job for you to showcase your talent. This could be the big break you've been needing."

Jordan studied Ellie. "You still haven't told us why you married Connor after how he treated you back in high school. And don't tell me he's changed."

Flustered by Jordan's question, Ellie took another sip of her champagne before setting her glass down. "Honestly, I don't know. I was shocked to find him in my bed the morning after. Neither of us remember all the details, but obviously we had some chemistry that night that made us do all kinds of crazy things."

Jordan tilted her head. "Like have sex?"

Ellie's cheeks flamed. She wasn't certain if she was more embarrassed that she didn't remember if they'd had sex, or if they hadn't had it at all. "I don't know."

Olivia's eyes rounded.

"Interesting," Jordan said as she pushed one of the presents on the table toward Ellie. "From me. Open it."

Relieved to have something else to focus on besides her mistakes, Ellie pulled the gold ribbon of the small rectangular box, then unwrapped the paper and opened it. She frowned down at the metal object inside. "Why would you give me handcuffs?"

Jordan's gaze was direct. "You did marry Connor Grayson. I figured handcuffing him to the bed might be one way to keep him by your side."

Ellie's breath hitched. "If he stays at the house with me, it'll be because he wants to be there, not because I forced him."

"That's a shame," Jordan said, "because he's even more handsome now than he was in high school."

"I agree," Olivia chimed in. "I met Connor a few months back. He has the most amazing eyes."

"I admit it—he's handsome, but can we please be serious?" Ellie groaned.

"The reality of the situation is that you're married. So what if you're not fully aware of all the details? Obviously, there's attraction between you two. Build on that." Olivia's hands moved to her own slightly rounded abdomen. She was three months along and had switched her Tuesday-night drink to seltzer water with a twist of lime in a champagne flute.

Ellie couldn't hold back a pang of jealousy over what Olivia had found: love, marriage, and a family. Her friend deserved them all.

"Open my present," Olivia encouraged, sliding the remaining gift in front of Ellie.

She shouldn't accept either one of these gifts. Pretending a joy she didn't feel, Ellie unwrapped the box and withdrew purple silk lingerie with lace appliqués at the bodice and hem. "It's exquisite."

Olivia beamed. "Enjoy being married, Ellie. It takes work, but all good things do."

Ellie tried to smile in return.

"Thank you, both of you, for the thoughtful gifts. No matter how silly someone's gift might be"—she cast a flustered glance at Jordan—"I do appreciate that you both want me to be happy." She knew what to do with the lingerie, but the handcuffs?

"I have a great idea." Olivia interrupted her thoughts. "Come with Max and me to a costume party at the Experience Music Project on Friday. Just the four of us. Since Max and Connor are friends, it should be really fun."

"We don't have tickets," Ellie protested.

Olivia waved her hand in a dismissive gesture. "Not a problem. I'll get two more. You're supposed to dress as your favorite movie couple. Please say you'll come."

"Am I invited, too?" Jordan interrupted.

Olivia leaned toward Jordan. "Sure."

Jordan reached for her phone and opened her calendar. A moment later she sighed. "Damn, I have to work."

Jordan worked long hours at the hospital. Ellie wasn't always sure if it was because she had to or because she wanted to, as an excuse. "Can't someone cover your shift?"

Jordan shook her head. "With it being the week of Halloween and a full moon, the emergency room will be busier than ever. This time of year we always have to staff up, not down."

"Next time," Olivia said with a reassuring smile.

"That sounds nice," Jordan replied with a hint of longing in her voice.

◆ ◆ ◆

Ernie kept his head buried in the newspaper for so long he thought his nose might be covered with black ink.

"Finally," Lenny nearly growled, setting his own newspaper aside as the three women left The Lucky Club. "I thought they'd never leave."

"Do you think Ellie recognized us?" Aaron asked.

Ernie folded his paper, grateful he no longer had to read the same page of the newspaper as he'd been doing for the past hour. "I don't think so, but I was nervous when her one friend studied us so closely. It made me want to get back into costume again. I can be invisible when I'm Elvis."

"In Vegas, yes," George admitted with a laugh. "In Seattle, not likely."

Aaron gave him a pinched look. "What are we doing sneaking around spying on the poor girl?"

George frowned at the man in the booth beside him. "What's wrong with you? You look like you just swallowed a lemon."

Aaron's sour look increased. "This isn't our style—"

"Boys," Ernie interrupted, his amusement fading. "We're making lemonade. Look what we discovered tonight by following Ellie here." He held up one finger. "She didn't talk to her friends about a divorce. If she was seriously considering that alternative, she would have told them." A second finger joined the first. "And she's going to a costume party on Friday. A costume party, boys."

All three of his friends' faces lit up, and George started to laugh. "It's not like the four of us don't have the perfect costumes to wear."

They all started to laugh.

"That's how we do our best work," Lenny managed to say.

"We learned something else as well," Ernie said, trying to bring the conversation back to a more serious tone.

"What's that?" George said, trying to keep his amusement in check.

"That pretty friend of hers with the dark hair . . . she needs a date."

George straightened, his laughter fading as he stared at Ernie. "Are you offering your services?"

"No," Ernie snorted. "I'm far too old for her. But who says we can't help her along that path? A pretty young woman like her ought to have lots of young men vying for her hand." Ernie frowned. "Do the young men still compete for a woman's attentions?"

Aaron looked thoughtful for a moment, then said, "Most of the couples who come to our chapel are well past the competition stage of their relationship. They are ready to commit to each other, however briefly."

"I'd be happy to help Jordan find the man of her dreams," George said with a grin.

"Just like we helped Ellie find hers," Lenny agreed with conviction.

Ernie couldn't help but smile. "Now that's more like it. No better way for the four of us to make ourselves useful than to not only help Ellie and Connor find their way, but help that pretty little Jordan polish some of her rough edges."

"Who says we have to change her?" Aaron asked.

"I like her fiery temper," George agreed.

"Boys," Ernie interrupted with a wave of his hands, "at least we are united in our purpose. Let's wait and see what opportunities present themselves. Okay?"

His friends nodded.

Ernie stood and withdrew a twenty from his wallet, tossing it on the table to cover the cost of four cups of coffee. As the accountant of the group, it was always up to him to see that the bills were paid. The expense of coming to Seattle seemed as though it would pay off in more than one way—as entertainers, friends, and now matchmakers to the lovelorn.

He'd worried that seeing Viola might churn up old memories that may have been better left undisturbed for them all. Instead, he could tell by the renewed spring in all their steps that the old excitement from years ago had returned.

For four single old men, it didn't get much better than that.

CHAPTER EIGHT

Staring out the parlor window, Ellie took several deep breaths, trying to calm down. Three days into the refurbishment of the house and they were facing a serious setback with the timeline of the exterior renovation. She'd lived in Seattle all her life, long enough to at least have considered that a typical October day was filled with liquid sunshine, as the locals often joked with each other.

Zanzibar sat in the windowsill, watching her with calculating gold eyes. Outside, rain drummed down from a steel-gray sky. Puddles formed on the street and in the grass, reminding her that this wasn't a passing shower. It had been raining all night and looked as if it would continue all day, or for the next forty days. It was hard to tell.

Would Connor head in to work today, or would he stay at the house? She was never certain from one day to the next. At the sound of footsteps in the hallway, Ellie knew she'd have her answer soon. "Good morning," she said a bit too brightly when Connor appeared in the doorway.

He wore jeans and a navy-blue T-shirt that could have passed for work clothes. On him, the fitted shirt looked sexy, revealing the corded muscles of his chest and arms beneath the thin fabric. He was supposed to be a geek who spent a lot of time in his lab, but he could have passed for a rugged athlete.

"Are you hanging out here today?" Ellie asked, surprised that she wouldn't come in second to his work.

"Yep." For a long moment he said nothing as his long and lingering gaze slid over her body, capturing her form beneath the unflattering sweatpants and long Mariners T-shirt she'd chosen with hard work in mind. Her hair was pulled back into a functional ponytail. She looked as dreadful as she knew how to look.

"Interesting outfit," he finally said, raising his eyes to hers.

"We were supposed to be painting outside." It was the only explanation she had, other than that she had to build some sort of barrier between herself and Connor. Every moment she spent in his presence, she could feel her resolve to stay unaffected by him melting. "Because of the rain, I thought we could take inventory of the furniture instead? We can figure out what needs to be moved into each room. Then we can prioritize the refurbishment based on what rooms will actually be open to the public for viewing."

"That's a great plan. I hadn't actually considered the fact we wouldn't be showing the entire house. It makes a lot more sense to determine what rooms will be open and which ones won't."

She smiled at the unexpected compliment. "In the end, staging the event will save us time and money. Wedding venues are an illusion created with a lot of plywood and duct tape, camouflaged by pretty flowers."

Connor laughed, the sound filling the room with intimate warmth. "I'm impressed. I should never have doubted your abilities."

For an hour they moved from room to room in the house, with Zanzibar following behind. In the master bedroom they discovered a closet full of Viola's old clothes. There were items Connor said he remembered, along with several ball gowns he didn't.

"I've never seen this many gowns in one place outside of a store," Ellie laughed.

"Me neither," Connor replied as they left the dresses where they were and moved on to the other three bedrooms on the second floor. When they were done, they headed to the family room downstairs.

On her clipboard, Ellie cataloged all the furnishings Viola had left behind. The three-story Victorian had six bedrooms, a library, music room, study, sitting room, kitchen, family room, dining room, four bathrooms, a ballroom, and a dumbwaiter that passed between the floors. While Grayson House was a small mansion by today's standards, it had been extravagant in its time.

"Most of the furnishings are antiques," Ellie said, clutching the clipboard in her hands as Connor moved alongside her in the family room. She dropped her gaze to her list. It was better to concentrate on the items there than on him.

At first she'd allowed herself to watch him, but that had been a mistake. There was a raw, masculine power that lived beneath his self-proclaimed geeky surface that anyone with eyes could see.

His green eyes had shifted from her. Now they returned, focused and intent. "It's hard living in a house full of priceless things."

"You lived here?" Her words were a little breathier than she would have liked.

He inclined his head. "After my mom left, Dad and I moved in with Grandmother. Dad kind of disappeared for a while. It was Viola who took care of me, but she had a lot of rules, especially when it came to the furniture."

Ellie could only imagine. Viola looked so soft on the outside—the woman within was another matter. "Did you live here long?"

Connor shifted closer as he inspected a lamp on the side table next to her. "About six years. That's how long it took for my dad to pull himself together. By the time he wanted to be a family again, I was eleven and rebellious."

His nearness felt like a flame down the side of her body. She frowned. "You were rebellious?"

He shrugged. "In my own way."

She fought to concentrate on what they were doing and not close her eyes and let her senses stretch. "What does that mean?"

"The best part of our new house was that it had a garage. I took it over and turned it into a laboratory. At first my dad argued that he wanted to park his car in there, but he finally gave in after I moved back in with Viola."

"You manipulated him." The thought gave her something else to concentrate on. She shifted away.

"I'm not proud of that fact, but yes. He let me set up in that private space where I conducted all kinds of experiments. It took me five years to figure out what I was good at—robotics. And I've never looked back."

"Are you and your dad close now?"

He let his gaze travel over the room, then looked back at her. "Not as close as I am to my grandmother, but we get along. I don't think we ever had a parent-child relationship. We're just two guys who are making their way through life."

"That sounds kind of lonely for both of you," Ellie said, meaning the words.

"We're fine." His expression shuttered as he turned away to study a bookcase up close. "What about you and your parents?"

She let out a dry laugh. "They meddle. They mean well, but there are two of them and one of me. I always felt like I was under an ever-watchful eye while growing up. One slipup and they would both come down on me."

When he glanced back, his control was back in place. "Does that explain the perfect grades you always tried so hard to achieve in high school?"

Ellie wondered what he was hiding. She'd obviously touched on a sensitive subject with her question about his father. Maybe in time he would tell her more. Letting things go for now, she answered his question. "I was terrified to disappoint my parents more than I already had."

He was beside her again. "You're not a disappointment, at least not to me." He reached for her shoulders, running his palms down her arms.

Her breath hitched. "You don't have to say things like that just to try and make me feel better." With barely a touch, he created a sensual tension within her that grew tighter and tighter.

"I'm not trying to make you feel better. I'm finally being honest with you and with myself. I know I hurt you eleven years ago."

"And I hurt you," she finally admitted.

"That doesn't mean we need to keep on hurting each other." His hands slid around her waist, drawing her closer.

Her heart thundered as his gaze dropped to her mouth. Without thinking, she parted her lips, and he laid claim. With only the lightest brush of his mouth against hers, she felt as though she were sinking, drowning, drunk with passion, captive to an exchange that was too potent for her excuses.

Tossing her better judgment aside, she kissed him back, demanding more, inciting what had simmered between them since the morning after their wedding, freeing herself of restraint.

And then his cell phone chimed.

Ellie froze as sanity cut through her desire.

Connor groaned. "I don't have to get that," he whispered against her lips.

"Yes, you do. Your grandmother is in the hospital," she replied, forcing herself to draw back.

Removing his hands from her waist, he waited another second before he fished his cell phone out of his pocket. "Hello?"

Ellie moved away, giving him privacy as she mentally reviewed a list of all the reasons why kissing him was a really bad idea. Kissing him would lead to other things, and when they parted, as per their agreement, she would be heartbroken again. Only this time it would be far worse, because she liked him far more than she should.

Instead of the boy from the past, an intelligent, sexy man dressed in blue jeans and a T-shirt stood in front of her, looking like the answer to a prayer. Uncertain what to do next, Ellie strolled about the room, jotting the furnishings down on her clipboard. Her gaze continued to stray to Connor.

After several long moments, he hung up the phone. "It was Viola. She wants us to come to the hospital."

"Is anything wrong?" Ellie asked with her heart in her throat.

Concern shadowed his features. "She wouldn't say anything except she wants to talk to both of us."

"I need to change my clothes. I'll make it quick." Ellie set her clipboard down.

Connor nodded. The moment between them was broken though not forgotten. She could see proof of that in Connor's eyes a moment before she raced up the stairs.

◆ ◆ ◆

Half an hour later, Ellie parked her car in the hospital parking garage. Connor couldn't help but worry as they made their way up to Viola's room, only to find she'd been moved from ICU to a PCU unit on a different floor.

He was thrilled his grandmother had improved enough to be moved, though it would have been nice to learn that information from the woman herself when she'd called. But that was Viola. She was an enigma, if nothing else.

Before they entered Viola's new room, Connor reached for Ellie's hand. "To keep up the charade."

Instantly her fingers curled around his. She offered him a gentle smile.

Connor returned that smile. Their marriage might be fake, but Ellie's caring about people was truly genuine. He could see that now that he'd let go of the past.

Inside the small, private room, Viola lay motionless in the center of her narrow bed. Her eyes were open, but her face was pale, almost gray. A heart monitor beeped in the corner, displaying a heartbeat that was steady and strong.

"Connor, Ellie," Viola said in a weak voice. At the sight of them, tears squeezed past her lashes and down her cheeks.

"How are you, Grandmother?" Connor bent down and placed a kiss on the older woman's forehead.

"I want you to start planning my funeral," her crackly voice replied.

Connor frowned. "You're getting better. It won't be long now before you're out of this bed and back to your weekly bingo nights with your friends."

The comment stopped her tears and earned him a wobbly smile. "You think so?"

"I know so." He had to sound positive. Viola still had a long way to go, but she'd always been a fighter. Connor stared down at the withered woman in the bed, so unlike his grandmother. Her dull, watery eyes blinked up at him. With his free hand, he reached for her fingers, wrapping them in his own. Hers were so slim, so fragile.

He swallowed past the lump in his throat. He wanted to make everything better, the way she always had for him—which was why he stood beside her bed with Ellie. Their marriage was going to give Viola the hope she needed to get well again.

Viola squeezed her eyes shut. "I'm so afraid." Tears once again slid down her temples.

Beside him, Ellie's lips thinned. She looked at Viola with suspicion but said nothing.

Connor frowned, not understanding her response to Viola's tears. He turned back to his grandmother and brushed the tears from her velvety cheeks. "You don't have to be afraid, Grandmother. You're not alone. You never will be."

"I wouldn't be so afraid if I had the hope of a great-grandchild." Her voice was a bit stronger.

Connor cringed at the look that now filled his grandmother's eyes. He knew that look. He'd seen it before whenever Viola wanted something to go her way. Is that what Ellie had been trying to communicate? That Viola was manipulating them? "Why the rush?" he asked with a hint of his own suspicion.

Viola pushed herself up on her elbows. "If you haven't noticed, I'm dying."

Ellie released a soft groan as she studied the pitcher and cup on Viola's side table with exaggerated interest.

"We've been married less than a week, Grandmother. We need to get to know each other before *that* happens."

"Then I suggest you speed the getting-to-know-you moments up," Viola said as she collapsed back against the mattress. "To that end, you're both going shopping today."

Ellie's gaze snapped back to his grandmother. "We need to work on the house."

Viola's weak eyes turned steely. "All newlyweds need china. I've arranged for you to pick out whatever you want at the downtown Macy's."

Ellie's face paled. "We don't need china. Nobody uses china anymore."

"Picking out china is an important part of any couple's new life together. If I can't have a grandchild right away, at least let me give you china." Her heart monitor beeped erratically, punctuating each word.

Connor suddenly felt a headache coming on. "Calm down, Grandmother," he said, knowing it was easier to comply than to argue. "What a generous gift. We're so pleased. Aren't we, Ellie?" He looked at Ellie expectantly. "You said the rain was a problem today. Why not stay inside and shop instead?" he urged.

Ellie released a sigh. "If it will make you happy, Viola, then, yes, we'll go shopping for china."

Connor was grateful for Ellie's capitulation. Eager to escape, he bent over his grandmother and kissed her on the cheek. He took Ellie's hand and ushered them both from the room before Viola could demand anything more.

Outside the room and Viola's hearing range, Ellie jerked to a stop, pulling her hand from his. "Why did we agree to something so absurd? We don't need china."

He gave in to the smile that threatened. "That whole scene was nothing but absurd," he laughed. "I never realized how manipulative my grandmother was."

Ellie stared at him a moment before the corner of her mouth tipped up. "You're just now realizing that? It was obvious from the beginning. Viola will do anything to get her way."

"Does she seriously think she can snap her fingers and demand a baby?" Connor asked.

"I think so," Ellie agreed. "And to punish us for refusing, we're forced to buy china." She raised her hands, palms up. "What are we going to do with such formal dinnerware?"

"Have a party?" he suggested. "Or we could throw it at each other before we get our divorce."

Ellie rolled her eyes. "Or we could leave it behind for Viola."

"Well, that's no fun." Connor's laughter continued as he held out his hand to her. "Want to go see what our options are?"

"You're talking about our options in china patterns, right?" she asked with a hint of a sparkle in her eyes.

"Of course."

She took his hand.

He curled his fingers around hers, feeling protective of the woman who was his temporary wife. He hadn't felt as protective of anything other than the onboard robotics in his self-driving car in years.

Having her around was turning out to be more dangerous than he'd imagined. He'd worried about his need to protect his heart in Las Vegas when he should have been worried about the memories she was churning up, the wounds she was healing, and just what would be left of their new china set over the next four and a half weeks.

CHAPTER NINE

After both Ellie and Connor had survived the daunting task of picking out a five-piece place setting for twelve, as Viola had demanded, Ellie finally relaxed in spite of the fact that there were now sixty pieces of china they would have to make room for in the house when they were delivered next week.

Ellie had been surprised how easy it had been for them to agree on a china pattern. They'd both liked the simple yet elegant silver ring around the outside edge of the plates, bowls, and cups. That they liked similar things shouldn't have pleased her as much as it did.

And when they were done picking out china, the saleswoman had informed them Viola had insisted on silverware and stemware as well. Choosing all of it had taken several hours.

"I promised you a date tonight," Connor said when they were done and had returned to his car. "How about an early dinner?"

"Sounds great. I'm starving," she agreed. They'd both decided just to keep shopping through lunch. Now that they were done doing Viola's bidding, it was with total satisfaction that Ellie slid into a chair at a table for two in the bar of the Bush Garden restaurant in Seattle's International District.

"Have you ever been here before?" Connor asked as he sat across from her.

"No," she replied, looking around the open room. The Japanese restaurant's subdued lighting and soft instrumental music helped dispel the last of her tension. "But I've heard the food is delicious and that they have karaoke music every night starting at five."

Connor looked at his watch. "Looks like we're just in time. Want to try a duet?"

"No," she said emphatically.

"Don't want to humiliate yourself at a public karaoke bar?"

"There is not enough alcohol in the world."

He sat back in his chair and studied her. "You'll get married drunk, but you won't sing drunk. What does that say about you?"

"Wouldn't you like to know?" She gave him an innocent smile.

"Hmm. The mysteries of Ellie. I like this game. I think it means you either had a bad experience singing or were humiliated in public. Which is it?"

She laughed. "Are you my therapist now?"

His brows drew together as he stared at her, as if putting together the pieces of a puzzle.

Ellie's breath caught. She could see the second his understanding dawned.

His eyes went wide. He sat forward. "I'm partially to blame for this, aren't I?"

The game was no longer playful as a flutter of apprehension worked up her spine. "Could we talk about something else, please?"

They were spared further conversation when the waiter came to take their order. After he left, Ellie took charge of the conversation. "There's something else we need to discuss."

"What is that?" Connor asked.

"It became very obvious to me last night when I met with Olivia and Jordan that we need a story to tell people. Like how we met. How long we've been dating. Why we got married in Las Vegas."

He considered her words. "You're right. We need something that makes sense to all our family, friends, and business associates—something that will help us when it comes time to end the marriage."

"Any suggestions?" she asked.

"We were abducted by four aliens who forced us to get married before they returned us to Earth." His grin was infectious.

She felt the corner of her mouth tug up. "The Elvises might very well have been aliens, but I doubt that story will fly with our parents."

"Yours seemed to accept that we are now together, without a lot of fuss." Connor paused while their server delivered a beer for him and a glass of water for her. Alone again, he continued. "Should we be worried about that?"

"No need. You heard my dad. He was beyond thrilled not to have to pay for a big, expensive wedding." Ellie grabbed her water glass. It wasn't much, but she needed something to hold on to in order to keep herself distracted from the way his smile turned suddenly charming, and the effect it had on her pulse. "The people I worry about most are our friends. Jordan and Olivia know we got married in Las Vegas, but they don't know we're only staying together for Viola's welfare."

"Then whatever we come up with will have to build upon what you've already told your friends." He paused, thinking. "How about this? We had a torrid love affair in Las Vegas. We decided we couldn't live without each other, so we got married."

"Too dramatic. How about this alternative? As friends in the past, we met up again in Las Vegas. Talking all night, we realized we missed each other, and in the spur of the moment decided to get married."

He laughed. "Most sane people would have only agreed to date, not get married."

She looked down at the ring on her hand. "We've already proven we're not exactly sane."

"I suppose so."

She offered a weak smile. "That we didn't do things the usual way will be why we separate after only five weeks of marriage. We didn't really know each other as well as we thought."

"It's close to the truth, and simple," he agreed. His eyes turned serious. "What other things could people ask us that we need to be united on?"

Ellie rolled her eyes. "Obviously about children, if we consider conversations we've already had with my mom and your grandmother."

"Your mom asked you about children?"

"She assumed that's why we got married."

His smile returned. "Okay, then . . . I want lots. Maybe ten, or why not a full dozen?"

Ellie choked on her own breath. "Not in this lifetime! Two will be plenty since we both have careers. You wouldn't expect me to give up my livelihood, would you?"

"Two is fine." He laughed.

A weighted silence had slipped between them again by the time the waiter brought their food.

"What other questions might people ask?" Connor continued when they were alone.

"Where we'll live? Where are we going on vacation this year since we didn't have a honeymoon? Did I take your last name? And a million other annoying questions."

He frowned. "That's none of their business."

She shrugged, digging into her beef sukiyaki with a pair of chopsticks. "It doesn't stop them from asking." Ellie knew, to the smallest detail, what her goals were in her professional life. She had short-term goals when it came to her Birthday Project. Yearly success goals. A five-year plan. In her personal life she had nothing, and she hadn't for a very long time.

"I say we just tell them to back off. Both of us refusing to talk about our plans can only work in our favor. It tells people without saying anything that we haven't thought our relationship through." He took a long sip of his beer before setting the mug down with a satisfied thump.

"Another way to get them not to even ask questions is to show them we know exactly what we want," he said.

"What exactly do we want?"

"Each other," he said with a smile that left her feeling slightly off balance. He pushed back his chair, abandoning his teriyaki beef steak, and headed toward the stage. Her heart nearly froze in her chest when, after consulting the technician at the electronics, Connor took the microphone.

"Before I start, I'd like to dedicate this song to my wife, Ellie. Thanks for the sheet music. It says it all," Connor said as the music queued.

The screen behind him filled with the words from Elvis Presley's "Can't Help Falling in Love." The karaoke words were displayed in big, bold letters, but Connor didn't look at the prompter or the screen, only at her. With total confidence and conviction, he sang a song about fools rushing in.

An older woman at the table beside her released a sigh, then turned to Ellie. "Hang on to that one, dearie."

What was he doing? They didn't need to put on an act for people they didn't know. But deep inside, a part of her she was unable to deny or control unfurled and started to melt.

Which was precisely the effect he'd intended.

Several other people at tables around her cast appreciative glances that said she was the luckiest person on earth. She had to admit, Connor was a catch—he was smart, successful, considerate, and determined to play his part. Which explained why he was onstage now. The show was only an act to impress everyone around them. So why was it working on her?

Connor sang about falling in love . . . with her.

An indescribable feeling of joy moved through her. God help her, she'd never felt this way before. Not even with Connor in the past. But was the lust and desire he stoked with a simple song worth the pain that would follow when they called it quits?

Could she risk everything, her heart, and definitely her sanity, by allowing the intimacy they'd planned so many years ago?

Sex and no commitments. Was she capable of that?

She swallowed roughly, considering her options as Connor finished his song. The crowd clapped and cheered enthusiastically as he took a bow. When he was done, he made his way back to her.

Decision time.

Did she clap for him, as everyone else did, or should she greet him with all the emotion his song had evoked? Her sensual self won the battle. She stood as he drew close, as his eyes connected with hers. Reaching up with both hands, she framed his face, moved into him, and kissed him with all the passion he'd stirred.

Over the pounding of her heart in her ears, she could hear the crowd cheering, but with the next heartbeat all noise faded away. If he wanted to pretend, she was his willing partner.

A thrill flashed sharp and bright through her. The kiss grew hungrier, more demanding, until she remembered where they were. With regret, she forced herself to pull away.

Ellie struggled to rein in her hunger. She drew a sharp breath, gathering her wits and her voice. "That was quite a song. Thank you."

Satisfaction flared in his eyes. "If that is to be my reward, maybe I should go sign up for another slot?"

"Or you should finish your meal so we can go home."

"That is the best idea you've had all day," he said with triumph in his voice. They both sat down and returned to their meals. Ellie ate without tasting a thing. The world around them had returned to normal. Another singer took the stage and sang a lively song that had the audience cheering once again.

But for Ellie, everything had changed because she could no longer back away. She wanted him for however long or short their time together might be. It wasn't wise. She knew she'd be hurt. But there suddenly didn't seem to be a force within her powerful enough to counter her desire.

As the crowd's enthusiasm for the performers grew, so did Ellie's desire to leave. They were headed back to the car when Connor's cell phone chimed again.

He looked at the screen. "It's Viola."

Ellie groaned, knowing there would be yet another demand imposed on them.

He answered as he stopped walking. "Hello, Grandmother. How are you?"

Ellie turned away and inhaled the rain-scented air, grateful for the moment to recover her composure. Passion still lingered in her blood, but distance from Connor helped the more rational, logical side of her brain kick in. The fact that Viola had called meant she and Connor would be off on another fool's errand before the night was through. What would it be this time?

She had her answer a few minutes later.

Connor ended his call and returned his cell phone to his pocket. "Viola has asked that we bring her a picture of the two of us that is not one of our wedding photos."

"You gave her one of those?"

He nodded. "One without an Elvis."

"She wants another picture tonight?"

He released a ragged sigh. "Yep. She wants something by her bedside to help her remember why she has to keep fighting."

"It's seven thirty at night. Where are we going to get a photo taken?"

Connor drummed his fingers on his chin a moment before his face lit up. "I know exactly where. It's a short trip from here. Come on." He held out his hand.

"Are we going to do this every time she calls?" Ellie asked, taking his hand, trying not to focus on the feel of his skin against her own.

"Until she's out of the hospital and recovering, yes."

Ellie could feel the echo of her desire in Connor's touch. This evening would have had a very different end had Viola not interrupted. Ellie still wasn't certain if she was happy about that or not. "Then we'd better go get that picture."

A few minutes later they pulled into the Uwajimaya parking lot. The Asian specialty store took up an entire city block and had been one of the key retailers in Chinatown since the end of World War II. The scent of roasting chestnuts and peanuts filled the air with a seasonal warmth as the two entered the busy store. Uwajimaya's downtown location wasn't just one store, but many smaller stores and restaurants joined under one roof. "How are we going to get a picture taken here?"

"There's a photo booth in the corner near the bookstore," Connor explained, making his way through the crowd of shoppers. "Have you ever been in a photo booth before?"

"No," she said with a laugh. "Have you?"

He shook his head. "There was never anyone I wanted to take pictures with . . . until now." At the photo booth, Connor added the necessary change, then pulled her inside and onto his lap. "Smile."

Ellie tried to concentrate on the task at hand and not on the width of the shoulders behind her, or the intimate way her bottom fit against his most male part. A wave of tempting warmth slid over her as the camera snapped pictures in rapid succession.

When the snapping stopped, he didn't set her away from him. He turned her around and placed a soft, gentle kiss on her lips—nothing like the kiss they'd shared at the restaurant, but it still kindled that flame. "We need to find a frame, then take the picture to Viola at the hospital."

She could only nod.

"I'll make everything up to you tomorrow," he said.

She raised a brow. "Is that a threat, Mr. Grayson, or a promise?"

His pupils dilated as a smile tugged at his lips. "Guess you'll find out tomorrow."

CHAPTER TEN

Thursday morning, Connor woke up to the sound of a hammer outside his window. "What the hell?"

He jumped out of bed. Still half-asleep, he staggered to the open window, only to startle the man on the scaffolding outside. Connor reached out and jerked the wobbling man back toward the house.

"Are you harassing my workers?" Ellie's sweet voice came from below.

Connor looked down at the base of the scaffolding to see Ellie wrapped in a heavy coat and scarf. She smiled at him, but behind that smile he could see the unappeased frustration that matched his own. Damn Viola and her phone calls.

"It's seven thirty in the morning," he replied, suddenly realizing his grip on the worker was unnecessary because of the safety harness strapped to his upper body. He released the man. "Sorry."

"No problem, sir. We got the all clear, so we assumed it was," the worker said in an apologetic tone.

Connor looked past him to Ellie. "You couldn't have waited another half hour?"

"Seattle city code states workers can begin residential construction at seven in the morning. We're on a tight timeline, remember?"

She was right. Yet that didn't make him any less frustrated or tired after spending yet another night at his lab after Ellie had gone to bed. He drew in a breath, hoping it would kick-start his brain.

The day was clear and cold. But at least the rain had stopped. If they were going to finish the renovation on time, they had to work quickly on the exterior of the house. "Why are the workers back here changing out the window frames so early?" he asked, pulling on a shirt.

The corners of Ellie's mouth tipped up. "The new windows will be here in about an hour. In order to be ready for them, the old, leaky, broken ones have to come out. The frames and all the wood with dry rot must be repaired."

"Sounds like you're on top of things," he conceded. There was no way he'd be able to go back to sleep now even though he'd been up half the night. He might have been at work, but his thoughts had all been on Ellie. "I'll be down to help in a few minutes."

"Don't hurry on my account," she replied. "I've got things under control."

He quickly dressed, then met her outside, where she stood directing the workmen. He had to admit—she did have everything under control. Two crews of two men each scaled the scaffolding near the back windows, each rigged with safety gear. Two more men sent up supplies or gathered the rotten wood pieces into bundles so they could be hauled away.

"Great work, guys. You'll be done in no time," Ellie encouraged before stepping back with a satisfied look.

"Seems like you picked the right contractors for the job," Connor said.

She startled at the compliment, as though surprised he'd noticed. "Thanks. It only took five years of working with contractors to figure out the best ways of dealing with them."

"You worked with contractors as a wedding planner?"

"Events coordinator," she clarified with a sigh. "Of course," she continued. "When a bride has a vision of her wedding, there's no changing her mind. If I couldn't find a venue that fit the bill exactly, then I built it. This is a step beyond the plywood-and-duct-tape method of wedding venues."

Connor looked around him. The work crews were happy, engaged, and definitely getting the job done. Her style seemed to be more one of motivation and praise than correction. Whatever magic she had was working on him as well. He was no longer tired, but eager to get started for the day. "I can keep an eye on the framing contractors if you want to go talk to the roofers. They arrived as I was coming back here. They're setting up at the front of the house."

"Thanks," she replied. "These guys know what they're doing, so you're mostly hanging around watching. Since you're co-foreman, they'll know to ask you if they have questions." With that, she disappeared around the side of the house.

◆ ◆ ◆

By lunchtime, the windows had been put in and all the roofing materials were perched on various sections of the roof, waiting to be installed. The roofers had said they needed two days to replace the roof. If the weather held, they might be done early.

"Want to go with me on an errand?" Ellie asked Connor later that afternoon when she found him at the front of the house replacing the old, rotting handrails that marched up the stairs. She gripped the left-side railing and shook it. It held firm beneath her grasp. "Good job, Grayson. You can build cars and railings." She graced him with a smile. "Who knew?"

That smile sent his heart thudding in his chest. "There's a lot about me you don't know."

"Maybe we should rectify that." The words seemed casual, yet he sensed they weren't.

"I'd like that," he replied. "Where are we going?"

"The paint store. We need to pick colors for the interior and exterior."

"I'll drive," he said, heading toward his self-driving car.

"No."

The word stopped him. He turned back toward her.

She gave him an apologetic look. "We only have an hour before the painters arrive. If you drive, it might take the whole hour to get there."

He laughed as he changed directions, heading for her gold MINI Cooper parked on the street. "You aren't the first person to tell me that. Don't worry. My car can go a lot faster, just not on city streets. The new artificial intelligence we're working on with Microtech will have us speeding along city streets just like all the other cars."

"When that happens," she said, getting into the driver's seat, "then we'll take your car. Until then, hop in."

Connor folded himself into the passenger seat. "Your car is actually smaller than mine."

"Yeah, but mine costs about a million dollars less." She started the engine and merged into traffic.

More like sixty million, but he didn't want to correct her. Continuing his research and development would be impossible without Microtech's additional $1 billion in support.

Ellie drove through the city and down to the industrial area of Seattle to a commercial paint store located along Fourth Avenue. Once in the store, she headed for a long row of paint chips and started selecting various shades of pink. "The Historical Preservation documents made it clear that in order to honor Grayson House's history we can't change the color of the house. We'll have to stick with the original colors of pink and white."

"Who knew there were so many restrictions," Connor said, studying all the pink paint chips in Ellie's hand.

"When dealing with a city's history and a dedicated landmark, lots of other people can get involved. We're lucky we aren't really changing anything, only fixing things up, or we'd never get the house done on time." Ellie moved on to the white paint chips.

He frowned. "Why don't you simply pick a pink one and a white one, and we'll call it good."

Horror reflected on her face. "Are you kidding? This is a huge task, picking just the right shade of pink and white. The colors will look different in the sun, or when the sky is gray. We must pick exactly the right ones."

Connor screwed up his face. "Really? They all look the same to me."

He realized his mistake too late. She grabbed him by the arm and dragged him over to the paint-mixing counter nearby. She laid each chip down on the beige laminate surface. "This pink has a hint of brown in it. While this pink is more of a salmon color. This is a ballerina pink, while this one is a flamingo pink."

Next she laid down the white paint chips. "All these whites are different as well. There are blue whites and gray whites and even whites with a hint of pink."

She drew one of the pinks down in front of the others, then drew a white paint chip beside it. "Here are the paints that match—Chantilly Lace for the white and Light Coral Sunset for the pink." She turned to him. "What do you think?"

"I think you don't need my help," he replied.

Surprise danced across her face. "Sure I do." She gathered all the unused chips back up and handed them to him. "You get to put these away while I figure out the interior colors. It would be a big help. Please?"

Connor stared down at the chips in his hands. He thought about all the times he'd given similar menial tasks to his staff members in their robotics lab. He never realized how stark the words sounded without the addition of the "please" at the end. "It would be my pleasure. I might actually learn something about color."

Twenty-five minutes later, all the paint chips were back in place, and Ellie had selected and ordered several other colors for the various rooms around the house. The delivery team would bring the paint to the house later that afternoon.

Back in her car, Ellie and Connor headed for Grayson House. "I know hanging out in paint stores is not your usual style. Thanks for coming." She smiled apologetically.

He shrugged. "Paint stores aren't my usual hangout, but look what I found." He pulled a paint chip from his pocket.

"The color of the front room? *Caliente* red?" she asked, turning to look at him.

"I never imagined I'd care what color the next car we build would be, but I'm really excited about this color."

She laughed. "Good heavens, what have I done?"

Connor grinned. "Created a monster, I suppose." Impulsively, he reached over and brushed a loose lock of hair behind her ear. It was something a lover might do.

Her eyes flared with desire a heartbeat before she turned back to the road. "You're not a monster. You're my temporary husband."

Her words made him feel a little dizzy. "Ellie," he said. When she glanced his way, he gave her his most dazzling smile. "There are things in our lives that are temporary, but some things are also very real. I'll show you just how real tonight."

"What do you have planned?"

"I'm not going to spoil that surprise. When it's time, you'll see."

◆ ◆ ◆

While Connor and Ellie were out of the house, George pretended to be a worker and slipped inside. Impersonating someone else was as natural to him as breathing. What wasn't so familiar was playing the role of matchmaker. What was taking Ellie and Connor so long to get together? Connor had found the sheet music about falling in love he'd left on his previous trip to the house and had acted on it by singing the song to Ellie. Ellie had no doubt found the flowers. What more was an Elvis to do besides serenade them himself?

George released a frustrated sigh. He'd try something else, one more time, before he'd give in to more drastic measures.

Without a doubt, he knew Ellie and Connor were attracted to each other. So what was holding them back from a true and lasting commitment? Silently, George crept up the stairs to Ellie's bedroom. If flowers and music hadn't worked, then maybe this next gift would.

Time was running short.

Viola needed a miracle, and by all that was holy, he and the rest of the team would give her one.

CHAPTER ELEVEN

The sky grew dark early in the Pacific Northwest in October. By five o'clock, the roofers came down and packed up their trucks. The painters finished sanding and had started sealing the cracks and holes in the exterior wood. Before the first stars came out, both crews had headed home for the night. Ellie had never been more grateful.

Since they'd returned from the paint store, she'd thought of nothing but the evening she'd spend with Connor. They'd each gone to their respective rooms to change and would meet downstairs again at six o'clock.

He'd refused to tell her where he was taking her, which made it difficult to decide what to wear. Ten minutes and five outfits later, she finally settled on black leggings, a gray sweater with black lace trim, black pumps, and a red neck scarf.

Connor was in the foyer when she arrived. He was dressed in khaki pants and a crisp white shirt. Ellie's eyes snagged on the vee of his shirt. It was open. Invitingly so.

She swallowed hard. Her gaze skidded up to his wet hair. He'd just showered. She could smell the light fragrance of soap mixed with Connor's own scent. It was a heady combination. Desire flared, making her breathing speed up.

"Ready?" Connor asked as he flicked on a flashlight.

"Where are you taking me?"

He held out his other hand to her. "We're going stargazing."

She crinkled her nose. "What?"

"Come, you'll see."

Ellie furrowed her brow when she looked past Connor to the grandfather clock. The sheet was gone. The old man looked at her with a question in his eyes as though asking what the heck she was doing.

She had no idea, but she didn't have to explain that to a clock. Turning her back on the old man, Ellie followed Connor up three flights of stairs to the attic. Once there, he dropped her hand and moved to the window. He set the flashlight so the beam shone back into the room; then he stepped out on the scaffolding.

"Where are you going?" Ellie moved toward the window.

He vanished. A moment later she heard a crinkling sound overhead as the blue tarp that lay across the roof was drawn back. Connor's head was visible through the three-foot hole. "The roofers aren't done, and they left us a wonderful spot to gaze at the night sky."

"What about rain?"

"The forecast calls for clear skies. But it will be cold as a result." Another moment passed, and he joined her once more in the attic, shutting the window behind him. From the corner of the room he picked up a blanket and handed it to Ellie. "You might need this. The heat is off in this room until the roof is sealed again."

The crispness of the night wrapped around them. The slivered moon hung high in the night sky, a scythe of gold. Grateful, she accepted the thick fleece blanket and wrapped it around her shoulders while he lit two candles on a side table. Soft, yellow-gold light dispelled the darkness.

"Aren't there any lights up here?" she asked.

"We don't want lights. They'll overpower the view of the stars. These candles will provide all the light we need." The warmth in Connor's gaze sent a shiver skittering along her flesh.

She looked up through the hole in the ceiling. The stars overhead glittered like diamonds. "I never realized you could see so many stars here in the city."

"We're far enough away from downtown that we get a fairly decent view. Magical, isn't it?"

"Yes," she replied, slightly breathless.

"Can you find the Big Dipper, also known as Ursa Major?"

"I remember something about the North Polar Star."

"The North Star is part of the Little Dipper, or Ursa Minor." He came behind her and pointed toward the night sky. "It looks like a bowl and a handle. Depending on the season of the year, the Big Dipper can be found in different places in the northern sky. Just remember, spring up and fall down. On spring and summer evenings, the Big Dipper shines highest in the sky. On autumn and winter evenings, it lurks close to the horizon."

"I see it now," she said, focusing on the horizon. With satisfaction, she turned to him. "I've looked up at the stars all my life without really seeing any of the constellations. Will you teach me more?"

"Anytime."

He took her hand and led her to a small table he'd obviously brought up for the two of them. On the table was a pizza box, a bottle of wine, and two wineglasses. "Dinner?"

He pulled out a chair for her to sit. Moving to his chair, he reached for the box, opened it, and turned it her way. "Only the finest for you."

He'd ordered black-olive pizza. Her favorite. A part of her delighted in the fact he'd remembered some small detail from their past. She accepted a slice while he opened the bottle of Chianti and poured them each a glass.

"So you wanted to get to know me better. I promise to answer any question you ask me tonight." He raised his glass for a toast.

She met his glass, took a sip, then set her wine back down, studying his face. He had soft crinkles in his skin near his eyes as he smiled at her. He smiled a lot. She'd always liked that about him. She liked a lot of things about him, as she'd been reminded over the past few days. "Anything at all?"

"Anything. Even if it's about the past."

She drew a breath and forged ahead. "If Viola has so much money, why were you so desperate to get a scholarship back in high school?"

He set his glass down and settled back in his chair. "I don't know much about Viola's finances, but I don't think she had access to her money until she turned seventy-two years old. That's when her annuities forced her to start taking withdrawals.

"When I was in high school, she had enough money to get by in this house, but not much more. She didn't have the funds to pay for college, and neither did my father. So when Harvard, Purdue, and Berkeley all wanted to talk about scholarships, I couldn't turn them down.

"I ended up picking Harvard, which offered a full-tuition scholarship for my undergraduate studies."

"That's quite an achievement," Ellie said, suddenly understanding the situation from his perspective. She'd wanted a date. He'd wanted a future. "I was unfair to you about the interviews. I see that now. Harvard was your dream."

Age and distance have a way of making some things clearer. Thinking about how to proceed, she studied the tiny dust particles that danced in the moonbeams overhead. "I didn't ever mean to come between you and your dreams. You're going to change the world with your self- driving car, Connor. Maybe what happened that night was for the best. Otherwise we both wouldn't be where we are now—you with your car, me with my events business."

"Can I ask you a question?"

"Seems only fair," she replied. "What do you want to know?"

"Is that why you became an event planner? So you'd be in charge and no longer waiting around for people to disappoint you?"

She drew back. "Wow. You don't pull any punches, do you?"

He shrugged. "It's just an observation."

And a little too close to the truth for her liking. Ellie laughed, the sound hard and brittle. "I do what I do to help others' dreams come true." She kept her head up despite the heaviness in her chest.

He tightened his fingers around hers. "I know we've gone about this whole relationship wrong, but can we be friends, now and after this is over?"

Ellie glanced down at the diamond ring on her finger. "Friends?" Could she be friends with a man she lived with, was married to, and wanted to have sex with? "We can try," she said past the thick lump in her throat.

"That's all either of us can do." He gave her a quirky, fleeting smile before he changed the subject. "Do you really think we can have Grayson House back to her former glory in the next four and a half weeks?"

It took her a minute to switch gears in her head. One minute they were talking like intimate friends; the next they were back to business as usual. "The hardest part of the renovation is the exterior. The crews are doing great work. The only thing that might hold us back is rain."

"The forecast looks favorable," Connor said between bites of his pizza.

Ellie looked through the hole in the roof. "You and I have both lived in Seattle long enough to know that could change at any minute." She returned her attention to the man across the table. "At least Viola budgeted for all the contingencies. If things start to look bad, I'll try to hire extra crews to get things done faster. At least the interior isn't weather dependent."

"But there's a lot of work on the interior, too, especially with refurbishing the furniture."

Ellie nodded. "I finally found the perfect craftsmen for that job. They start tomorrow. They'll focus on the wood, and I'll get busy with the fabrics."

"It sounds like everything is under control," he said, sipping the last of his wine. He lifted the bottle to refill their glasses, then frowned at her nearly full glass. "You're not drinking tonight?"

"I'm a little distracted by other things," she admitted.

He set the wine down. "By me?"

"Yes." The word faded away; all that remained was the soft creaking of wood and the whisper of the wind as it swirled around the attic.

He stood and came around to her side of the table. Offering his hand, he helped her up, pulling her close until she could feel the slow warmth of his breath brush her cheek. The silence that hovered between them seemed charged with invisible sparks. He reached up and touched her cheek.

She went hot, then cold at the gentleness of his touch. Giving herself over to the moment, she leaned in and brought her lips to his. As if by their own volition, her hands slid up his chest and locked behind his neck.

In response, his arms moved around her, settled in the hollow at the base of her spine, then pulled her close.

Chilly night air swirled around their bodies, as though rejoicing in the fact they'd joined together. It felt so good, so *right* being in his arms.

His tongue slipped through her parted lips and touched hers. At the contact a jolt of pure fire went straight to Ellie's core.

He broke the kiss. "Does this mean what I hope it means?"

Ellie felt the deep timbre of his voice clear down to her toes. "I want you. I won't deny that."

"And yet you hesitate."

She'd had casual sex before, but nothing more. Ellie had never had that "something special" her friend Olivia talked about with anyone except the man in her arms. Would giving in to him now ruin her for anyone else?

She swallowed roughly and tried to concentrate on anything other than Connor's full lower lip. Or the feel of his heartbeat against her chest.

Perhaps it was time to satisfy the need that never seemed too far away when he was near.

On that thought, she met his stormy green eyes. "I don't want to hesitate any longer."

"Thank God," he breathed as he captured her lips.

Her lips moved over his, hot and demanding. Her senses were swimming, the ability to think clearly ebbed, and she lost herself in a maelstrom of desire.

An onslaught of pent-up emotions and forbidden passion swamped her. Needing an intimate connection, she pulled him toward her.

As his hips pressed against hers, she fit herself against his hardening arousal, and every cell in her being came alive.

Connor groaned and pulled back, his breathing ragged. "Before we go further, we are agreed this is for fun, right?"

"Yes," she whispered.

"I don't want to disappoint you. I care about you, but I have no room in my life for commitment or a relationship. I'm already married to my job."

Her mind still swirling with desire, she nodded. "I get it. Would you just shut up and kiss me?"

And he did exactly that.

He kissed her with a thoroughness that sent her senses spiraling as he moved back to the westward wall, pulling her with him. Easing his hand under her sweater, his fingers skittered across her sensitive flesh, across her abdomen, along her sides, until he found and cupped her breasts atop the sheer fabric of her bra. Warm, demanding fingers sculpted her every curve, possessing her.

She succumbed to only sensation, to the unrelenting desire that pulsed through her veins.

Their veins.

No longer resisting, she reveled in the knowledge that she could still lure him, arouse him, incite him to action. A thrill of expectation flashed through her, bright and hot.

His kiss grew hungrier, more demanding.

Maybe it was the culmination of the last eleven years that seized them now, sent them into this flurry of desire. Or maybe they were finally at the right time and the right place in their lives to act on their dormant passion.

Ellie no longer cared about the reason, only that they were finally free from their restraints, together. She let her hands trail along his sides and then farther down until she sank her fingers into his buttocks, curling her body intimately against his, moving seductively.

Breaking the kiss, Connor reached for the hem of her sweater and pulled it over her head. Next he stripped her leggings away. Her breath hitched, not at the chill in the air, but at the warmth of Connor's gaze, at the heat spiraling through her as she stood bared before him.

He let her undress him, and as she did, his lips curved into a seductive smile. He made no move to touch her until he stood naked before her, bathed in the moonlight that limned every muscle, every taut line of his face.

His chest swelled as he took a sharp breath; then slowly, deliberately, he brought his hands to her waist and lifted her up, caught the back of her thighs, spreading her wide, then stepped into the nakedness between them.

The hardness of his body pressed against her as she looped her arms around his neck. Reckless abandon pounded in her blood as she locked her legs around his waist. He explored her skin with his hands and his lips until she burned, until need was a molten ache low in her belly. She tilted her hips forward, wanting, needing, what he offered.

He drew her hips toward his until the broad head of his erection parted her slick folds, and he pressed in, possessing her as though their past had been another lifetime ago.

Her breath shattered as he thrust inside. Surrendering fully, she gripped his shoulders, then tipped her head back, closing her eyes, letting sensation after sensation wash across her nerves. He was hot and hard, and he filled her fully.

He lifted her bottom, spreading his fingers across her smooth flesh as he drew his erection from her sheath only to slide back in again. He penetrated her deeply until her breath came in panting gasps, matching his.

Every nerve sparking with pleasure, every muscle tightening, tensing, she cried out and plunged over the edge. Ripples of her climax caught him in its power and echoed through him. The mingled sensations continued, racked through them, until they both floated in the aftermath.

He leaned back against the wall, taking her with him in a tender embrace, still joined in the most primitive way. His chest rose and fell as he pulled her protectively into his arms, cocooning her against his chest. She concentrated on his heartbeat as it gradually slowed.

Together they drifted back to the reality of the night. The chill air touched her now, pebbling her nipples and cooling her overheated flesh.

◆ ◆ ◆

After a long while, Connor finally managed to summon the strength to lift Ellie from him. He set her on her feet. Reaching down, he drew her abandoned blanket back over her shoulders to shield her from the cold.

He'd always been a little egotistical and stupid when it came to Ellie.

He'd been egotistical in that he actually thought he could have a physical relationship with her for fun. The stark reality stared at him now with wide brown eyes. Because now that he knew the pleasures of her body, he wanted more.

And not just for fun.

He'd been stupid in the fact that he'd wanted her so badly he'd forgotten to protect her.

"Ellie, I'm so sorry," he said, his breathing harsh and ragged. "I didn't use a condom. Are we okay?"

Her eyes flared momentarily before they shuttered against him. "It's fine. Don't worry about it."

But it wasn't fine. He could feel her drawing back. Desperate to maintain the closeness they'd shared, he reached for her hands. "If anything was to happen, please know I would take care of you."

"That wasn't in our agreement." She looked away. "Let's just enjoy what we had and what we'll continue to have and let everything else just take care of itself."

She was shutting him out. He should be happy she only wanted to have fun. He opened his mouth to respond, then froze when the air around them split with an unearthly shriek.

Ellie bent down and scooped up her clothes. "What was that?"

The sound came again, this time from overhead. Connor looked up to see Zanzibar staring at them through the hole in the roof. "How did you get up there, you crazy cat?"

Connor dressed in a rush, intent on rescuing the beast. He moved back to the window and once again scaled the scaffolding.

Zanzibar waited quietly for Connor to scoop him up. "Here," he called to Ellie below. "Take the cat while I cover the roof again."

Ellie appeared below the hole with a frown on her face. "That cat hates me. I don't know about this."

Connor lowered the cat down.

Zanzibar meowed—the sound somewhere between an angry warning and a plea.

"It'll be fine," Connor assured her. "Just grab him and hold him next to your body. Cats like that."

Begrudgingly, she took the cat between her hands as Connor turned away to drag the tarp back over the hole and secure it from the wind and rain. When he made his way back through the window, he paused, surprised by the scene.

Ellie stood in the middle of the room, fully dressed. Zanzibar sat dutifully at her feet.

"He doesn't look like he hates you," Connor said, coming inside and sliding the window closed.

"We came to an agreement." She bent down and picked up the cat, thrusting him into Connor's arms.

A lock of honey-colored hair fell from her ponytail against her temple, loosened no doubt by their lovemaking. Connor wanted more than anything to tuck the strand behind her ear. Instead, he tightened his hold on the cat.

"Let's call it a night," Ellie said with a yawn. "You take Zanzibar downstairs. I'll clean up here."

"Stay with me." The sentiment escaped before he thought about what he was saying. He paused, frowning. Those words were not light and carefree, or anything close to what he should have said as part of their temporary relationship.

In response, Ellie merely raised a brow, stacking their plates with one hand and scooping up their glasses and the wine bottle with the other. "Tomorrow will be a busy day if the rain holds off. Now that *that's* out of our system, take the cat and go to bed."

Not one damn thing was out of his system. The two of them had finally been thrust into the fiery inferno they'd always hovered on the brink of before. He could still feel with stunning clarity how she felt as she took him into her body, the feel of her hands on his overheated skin, burning him, branding him.

Ellie met his aching, desperate gaze with a satisfied smile. "Good night, Connor."

Good night? Not likely, not when he held a cat in his arms instead of the woman who was his wife.

CHAPTER TWELVE

The next day Ellie kept herself busy with the contract crews she'd hired. By the end of the day, the roof was finished, the exterior of the house was complete, and the entire first floor now sported fresh paint. The parlor and music-room walls were a rich red, while the rest of the rooms and hallways were a calming taupe as evidenced by the paint on her clothes, skin, and hair.

A good kind of exhaustion settled into the aching muscles of her neck, arms, and shoulders as she made her way upstairs. She had one hour to get out of her painting clothes and shower before she and Connor had to leave for their date with Max and Olivia tonight.

In her room on the dresser, she found an envelope, sealed with wax. With anticipation, she broke the seal and slipped the single sheet of paper from inside. She read the bold, slanting script:

> *Let old griefs be gone*
>
> *let us start anew*
>
> *once you accept how much I love you.*

"How much I love you?" Why would he write something like that to her and not tell her to her face? Did he mean the words, or had he meant "I love you as a friend"? Or had he noticed her distance and was trying to make unnecessary amends for an imagined slight?

She fell onto her bed with the note in hand. She hadn't given him the chance to have a true conversation. All day she'd pushed him away, shielding herself and her emotions, uncertain if she wanted to pursue a physical relationship with him or try to keep her distance. She'd given him tasks that kept him in other parts of the house. Every time he'd finished that task and tried to talk to her, she'd found another urgent thing for him to do.

Had he been trying to tell her this all day? No one had ever said those words to her before . . . or written them either. How had they gone from pretending to be married to this in such a short time? She hadn't considered that they would ever feel more than a strong attraction to each other. But love?

Ellie brought the note down to rest against her chest, feeling her heart beat a little bit faster beneath her hand. Until Connor said the words to her directly, she couldn't quite believe they were true. Maybe he would say them tonight. She drew a slow, even breath that cleared her head. Time would tell. In the meantime, she needed to take a shower and slip into her costume.

She'd bought a costume for Connor as well and had left it on his bed. At the thought, she smiled. What would he think of her choice, and more important, would he wear it? She'd find out soon. With thoughts of his poem filling her head, she headed for the shower.

Exactly one hour later, she hurried down the staircase to meet Connor in the foyer. The heated spark in his eyes told her he approved.

He was dressed in black jeans and a black T-shirt with the sleeves rolled up over his biceps, and he had a black leather jacket hooked by one finger draped over his shoulder. He'd slicked his hair back. The man was drop-dead gorgeous dressed as Danny Zuko from *Grease*.

And when he swaggered toward her, her knees went weak. "Hello, luscious," he said in a deep, evocative voice as he raked a hungry look over her body. "Nice costume."

She swallowed roughly. Maybe she hadn't thought this through. As Sandy to his Danny, things between them were already heated, and they hadn't even left the house. "There's still time to change into something else if you'd prefer," she offered.

"And give up seeing you in skintight black leather? Not a chance." He pulled her into his arms and gave her a sizzling kiss. Her body flared in response. And with one kiss, all her good intentions fell around her feet.

The man was temptation himself.

His tongue explored her mouth with leisure as his hands smoothed the silken back of her off-the-shoulder body-hugging top. Then, he bent down and scooped her off her feet and into his arms.

"Connor," she gasped as he carried her effortlessly out the door toward a sleek black Corvette that waited by the curb. With his boot he opened the passenger-side door and set her gently inside. "Your car?"

His green eyes were alive with humor and hunger. "Borrowed from a friend. We couldn't show up as Sandy and Danny to a party driving any fuel-efficient or robotic car, now could we?"

"I suppose not," she replied with a laugh as a thousand other emotions tore through her. "But how did you know what costumes I bought?"

He raised a brow. "I'm not as unobservant as you think." He closed her door, strode around to the driver's side, and got in. The car started with a low hum. He put the stick shift into gear, and they headed away from the residential area, toward the city's center.

It was all she could do not to reach out and touch him. Instead, she focused on the road and the fallen leaves that swirled through the air. It was clear and cold, but with Connor near and dressed like he was, she doubted she'd feel anything but overheated all night.

When they arrived at the Experience Music Project, Connor dropped the car at valet parking, offered on the lower level. He came around to her door and helped her out. Through the open doorway of the oddly shaped metallic building, the pulse of music drew them inside.

Olivia and Max were waiting for them in the lower lobby, dressed as Buttercup and Westley from *The Princess Bride*.

Olivia rushed forward and folded Ellie in a hug while the men shook hands. "Oh, Ellie, you guys look amazing as Sandy and Danny!" she exclaimed.

"How fitting you chose the destined-to-be-together-forever lovers Buttercup and Westley. Couldn't be more perfect," Ellie said over the music.

"Actually, this costume was the only one that hid my baby bump," her friend replied close to her ear. "Max wanted us to go as Batman and Catwoman," she said loud enough for all to hear.

"Were they ever a couple?" Connor asked as they headed for the stairs that would take them to the main floor and the Sky Church, where the costume party was in full swing.

"Yes," Ellie and Olivia replied at the same time. Laughing, they continued up the stairs.

The spacious room on the main floor known as the Sky Church was crowded. The sound of voices and pulsing music enveloped them. Colored lights shone down on what looked like oversize, upside-down umbrellas that hung from the ceiling, saturating the entire room in blue for several minutes, then red, then green, then orange.

When Max and Connor walked away to get drinks, Olivia turned to Ellie, the ever-changing colors of the room reflecting off her crown. "How are things? You look great, happy, even. Is everything with the house going well? Is married life everything you thought it would be?" Her friend asked the questions in a rush.

"Things are on track with the house. The weather finally cooperated, and the exterior is done. Now all we need to do is focus on the interior and the decorating over the next several weeks."

"And the two of you?" Olivia asked with a quirk of her brow. "I have to admit, Connor looks quite yummy in black."

Too yummy for her own good. "I'm having fun. That's what I want for now."

Relief crossed Olivia's face. "I'm glad to hear that. I was a little worried about how quickly you got married, but I have to admit, you really look like this arrangement agrees with you."

Arrangement? Ellie swallowed past the lump in her throat. Olivia had no idea how close to the truth she was.

Olivia narrowed her gaze, suddenly seeing too much. "And the sex? Is that okay as well?"

Ellie straightened and looked from side to side to make certain no one else had heard such a personal question. "Yes. That's better than fine. It's been amazing." At least she didn't have to lie about that. Just everything else.

Olivia bumped Ellie with her shoulder. "Good. I'll stop being your mother."

Ellie bumped her back. "It's nice to know you care." She sighed. "My mother never asked about our relationship. She was far too busy letting me know how happy she and Dad were to get me off their hands."

"Seriously?" Olivia laughed.

Ellie gave her friend a droll look. "Oh, yes. They booked a cruise with the money they'd saved for my wedding."

"It could be worse," Olivia offered, always trying to find the bright side to everything.

"It is worse. I didn't marry only Connor. I married his grandmother as well."

"Max mentioned Viola was a feisty one. Is she critical of you?"

As best friends, Max had no doubt spent plenty of time with Connor's grandmother. "No," Ellie admitted, "but she's demanding."

Olivia's expression softened. "Aw, she'll warm up to you. How could she not?"

"I hope you're right, before she moves into Grayson House with us."

Olivia cringed. "That's not the best way to start a new marriage."

Neither was the way she and Connor had entered into their pretend marital bliss. Ellie looked away, no longer able to meet Olivia's questioning gaze. "The guys are back," she said, relieved to see Max in his swashbuckler black and Connor in his 1950s bad-boy attire, carrying beverages for the four of them.

Connor slipped in beside her and kissed her cheek before handing her a seltzer with a twist of lime.

"How did you know I like seltzer and lime?" Incredulousness laced her voice.

"Max told me you like seltzer or pink champagne," Connor admitted. "And since they don't have pink champagne . . ."

"This is perfect. Thank you."

Olivia watched the exchange with a raised brow but said nothing. For the rest of the evening, it was Ellie's turn to watch how affectionate and in love Max was with her friend. Clearly the two of them had found their perfect match.

Ellie's observations were interrupted when Connor extended his hand to her. "Dance with me?"

She accepted his hand, desperate in that moment to experience some of the same magic Max and Olivia had found. All around them costumed dancers undulated to the beat.

A moment later, a new song started, one with a much slower tempo. Ellie narrowed her gaze on the man before her. "Did you do this?"

"Not unless the DJ was reading my mind," Connor replied, pulling her close for a slow dance. "Let's just believe destiny is intervening on our behalf."

Ellie wasn't sure she believed in destiny, but she was willing to embrace the concept, however temporarily, if it kept her in Connor's arms tonight.

They danced through several songs and had just started another when a pretty, dark-haired woman dressed as Olive Oyl approached. Except this wasn't the frumpy, wear-her-heart-on-her-sleeve Olive Oyl depicted in the cartoons. This rendition wore a low-cut red blouse, a black miniskirt, and thigh-high boots that made her legs look long and sexy.

"Connor Grayson. What are the chances of us meeting?" the woman asked with what seemed like a genuine look of astonishment.

"What are the chances?" Connor said, his voice hard as he flipped up the collar of his leather coat. His stance changed, and Ellie was convinced he tried to make himself look intimidating. Connor's lips thinned. "I'm just here dancing with my wife."

"Wife?" the woman said with disbelief.

"Amanda Frost, meet my wife, Ellie Grayson."

Ellie didn't extend her hand, and neither did Amanda. They simply glanced at each other with a civil nod of acknowledgment and, if Ellie were honest, a tinge of jealousy on her part. She'd dressed to attract Connor's attention tonight. Yet the woman before them was far sexier in her modified Olive Oyl costume.

"How do you two know each other?" Ellie asked, not really sure she wanted to hear the answer.

"Amanda was my college girlfriend and the woman who stole the plans for my onboard GPS tracking system."

Amanda's perfect face hardened. "You could never prove that."

"That you started your own robotics company tells me all I needed to know." He shrugged. "That intelligence you stole is antiquated now. I've developed something much better. So, I should really thank you for pushing me to better my own best."

"I didn't steal from you," she objected. "Tiny Byte has its own development staff. We have our own technology, and we're going to be first to market with our self-driving car design."

Connor shrugged once again. "Sooner or later the better technology will prove itself."

Amanda cursed. "You really get off on being such a know-it-all, don't you, Connor?"

"It's not being a know-it-all. It's solid science, research, and testing. It's not about cutting corners; it's about total dedication."

Amanda glared at him.

"You know, I do remember reading something about the two of you getting married in Las Vegas. Vegas? Really? You couldn't wait for a real wedding?"

In response to the woman's flippant remark, Ellie said, "Of course I married Connor in Vegas. I wanted to snatch him up before someone else got to him. The man's a sexy, gorgeous hunk. I'm smart enough to know a good catch when I see one."

Amanda snorted. "I don't see it."

Wanting to drive her point home, and maybe cause the other woman a twinge or two of her own jealousy, Ellie turned to Connor, stepped close, and gave him a sizzling-hot kiss. His arms went around her, pulling her close. Despite the fact that the kiss was for show, her body instantly flared in response. When she stepped back, Connor's green eyes danced.

"Well, isn't that cute?" Amanda said snarkily. "You two look like you deserve each other."

Ellie continued staring up at Connor, smiling sweetly, letting Amanda's barbed words wash over her. "Are you ready to go home, husband? I find I suddenly can't wait to remind myself of how sexy you really are."

Connor's gaze shifted to Amanda. "You've got to love a woman who can't wait to get you naked."

Ellie's cheeks flamed.

Amanda choked.

Connor said nothing more as he wrapped his arm around Ellie's shoulders, leading her toward Max and Olivia.

"Was it serious between you two?" Ellie asked Connor after they moved to the opposite side of the room. Ellie watched as the long-legged woman went back to the guy who was most likely her date, if the Popeye costume was an indicator. The man was older than Amanda by at least twenty years, bald, and pudgy.

"For a time, yes," Connor admitted. "On paper, Amanda and I were extremely compatible. Like me, she's smart, driven, and competitive. In the end, all the things that attracted me to her destroyed any chance at a relationship we might have had."

"She stole your work?" Ellie asked, glancing at Connor's ex-girl-friend out of the corner of her eye.

"Without a doubt." Connor's voice fell to a harsh whisper. "But as she said, I had no proof. It was my word against hers."

Ellie turned back to face Connor fully as a flutter of panic moved through her. "Are you worried about Amanda stealing your work again? You said you were close to a breakthrough on your car. Could she know that?"

Connor's jaw set. "I'm wise to her tricks and have excellent security at the lab. The university implemented a state-of-the-art biometric system to keep our development secrets safe. Amanda would have to do something pretty drastic to walk away with my prototype this time."

Ellie's gaze strayed back to Amanda, who was looking at them as if she was trying to figure something out. That's what worried Ellie. The sexy, smart woman looked entirely capable of doing something drastic.

"Ellie." The sound of Connor's voice brought her attention back to him. "Let's not let Amanda ruin this night for us." Leaning closer to her ear, he whispered, "Did you mean what you said a few minutes ago?"

A shiver went through her as his breath brushed her overheated flesh. Pulling back to look him in the eyes, Ellie replied, "I meant every word."

"That's my girl," he said with a devilish smile as he planted a kiss on her lips that made her weak in the knees.

When he finally broke the kiss, she slumped against him. "What was that for?"

"For wearing those tight leather pants tonight. I held off as long as I could, but when you called me sexy, I lost control."

She laughed. "You can lose control anytime, gorgeous."

"First I have to get you home. Then watch out." His eyes flared before he scooped her off her feet, carried her down the flight of stairs, out the door of the museum, and back to the car.

As they sped off down Mercer Street, Ellie was extremely grateful Connor had borrowed his friend's very fast car.

CHAPTER THIRTEEN

Ellie had called him a sexy, gorgeous hunk in front of Amanda, whose gasp of surprise still warmed Connor's heart. Needing a connection to the woman beside him, Connor laid his hand on Ellie's leather-clad thigh.

At his touch, Ellie turned to him. In the moonlight pouring through the windows, her eyes glimmered with appreciation and raw lust, making the ride home from the party pure torture. He kept to the speed limits on the streets, but if they didn't arrive at Grayson House soon, he was certain he'd erupt into flames.

He should be wondering why Amanda had suddenly reappeared when she lived out of state. He'd always been happy about them living so far apart, especially since they ran in the same social and professional circles. He'd been able to avoid her at conferences over the years, but tonight their paths had crossed once more. It might behoove him to figure out why. Those thoughts were cast aside as Connor remembered the way Ellie had looked up at him, the way she'd kissed him, as if she truly cared about him.

He drove a little faster.

As soon as they stood inside the house and the door closed behind him, he scooped Ellie into his arms as he had earlier. Only this time he pounded up the stairs to the master bedroom. He set her on the bed on her back, then plucked off her black stilettos, tossing them aside.

"You're very sexy tonight," he said. Looking at her made him hard, and desperate to appease the need racing through him—need that had sizzled to life the moment she'd walked down the stairs tonight.

"And you're wearing too many clothes, Mr. Grayson," she said. There was a smile in her eyes, a smile he'd grown to appreciate this week, more than he'd thought he could. A smile he would miss when this flame of theirs ended.

Connor kicked off his boots and tossed them beside her shoes. The rest of his clothes followed in a rush, thrown down as his temperature spiked even higher at the sight of her creamy breasts rising and falling above her sweetheart neckline.

He crossed to the bed and knelt down beside her. He touched the bare flesh of her arms. Her breath caught as she waited, ready to follow his lead. He bent his head and kissed her—a soft kiss, slow and gentle. This kiss was freely given on both sides, a kiss that allowed their mutual passion to burn.

His arms locked around her as she pressed against him, into him, wrapping her arms around his neck. His tongue dueled with hers, explaining without words how much he needed her, wanted her, desired only her tonight.

She read his message and, in response, traced the muscles of his back with her hands, possessing every inch of him, stroking and arousing.

He closed his eyes, reveling in the sensations chasing through him. His heart raced in his chest at the promise in her touch. A powerful current stretched between them, dispelling rational thought, leaving them with only hunger and desire and that indefinable something more. It was that unnamed element that rose up in him, filled him, and flowed into her.

Ellie groaned and writhed beneath him as his hands possessed every inch of her body, every curve. She willingly accepted what he offered, allowing it to suffuse every inch of her skin, right into her bones.

Connor broke the kiss and pulled back. He opened his eyes, studying her face—seeing her need but also her response to his touch. Brown eyes filled with heat as well as appreciation.

Swept away by a relentless tide, he tenderly pulled the edge of her top from her waistband. He slid his hands beneath to find her heated flesh as he shimmied the fabric up and over her head. A quick release of her lacy bra, and her breasts were freed to his touch.

Her lips curved up with need and anticipation that sent his pulse drumming. He reached for the zipper along the side of her skintight pants. He released the fabric's caress against her soft skin, replacing its possession with his hands. He slid her pants down her legs, slowly exploring the length of them, caressing and possessing until she was freed of all obstacles and his world became only her.

Everything around them grew silent except the creaking of the old house and their mingled breathing. Connor reached for a box at the bedside and hurriedly rolled a condom over his erection. Protected at last, he drew her body full against his. Her soft, womanly weight molded against him, and her nakedness sent a jolt of heat to his very core. He felt himself throbbing, flexing against the firmness of her thigh. He inhaled her scent—wildflowers and sunshine. She smelled too good. She felt too soft.

"When I first woke up in Vegas and saw you standing above me, I wondered what I'd done in this life to deserve such punishment."

She tensed.

"I was wrong," he continued. "The punishment was you not being in my life."

She drew back, studying his face. "What are you saying?"

"I'm not sure, exactly," he admitted. "But this, whatever this is, feels like the first honest thing between us in a very long time."

There was so much more he wanted to say, yet he couldn't force the words past his lips. When her brown eyes met his, he saw in their depths a connection so deep it filled his chest with warmth. Neither of them knew what their future held beyond this moment. But they had this moment. He had to make that count. Letting all else slide from his mind, he brought a finger up to her lips. Gently, rhythmically, he stroked circles around their fullness. He feathered his fingers down her arm, to her fingers, stroking each one as though memorizing every nuance of her body.

He trailed his touch across her hips, the flat of her stomach, and upward, tracing the underside of her breasts. Moving slowly, he palmed them. He closed his hands around her flesh, and the flames inside him leaped even higher. He stroked, sampled, and caressed until her breath shuddered, until his own skin burned, until need ached inside him like a molten fire.

Giving in to that urgent need, his own raging desire, he moved over her, spreading her thighs, settling between. His hips cradled hers. Her welcome heat drew him forward until he thrust in.

Her body arched under his, accepting all he offered. She climaxed at his entrance, but he'd never let her settle for that. There was so much more to offer her tonight.

Connor moved within her, each stroke deliberately stoking the flames. The moan she uttered was music to his ears, encouraging him on, spinning them both into an all-consuming, rapturous spiral.

Lost to all else, he continued the driving rhythm that would be their salvation. Over and over he filled her until their mingled breath came in panting gasps, until he felt himself tightening toward that senses-stealing moment.

Then he came apart, taking her with him into the rippling cascade of their release. His senses shattered, stretched, and finally floated on a plane of complete satisfaction.

A quiet, tender moment passed as his heartbeat slowed and the glow faded. His arms gave way, and he slumped over her, coming down on his elbows. Finally he withdrew to shift to the side. Her heated flesh pressed against his, and he felt her heartbeat in a similar cadence to his own, both comforting and evocative.

They lay together for what might have been minutes or hours until he summoned the strength to draw up the covers and rearrange them in his bed.

Ellie stirred. "I should go back to my room."

"Stay," he responded, unsure if he meant for the night or forever, as his senses were still raked raw. "Let me hold you awhile."

Satisfaction flared in her eyes as she snuggled into his arms. He buried his face in her hair, breathed the sweet scent of it. A wave of fierce possession tore through him. He'd never felt anything like it before. He wasn't certain where it came from, but it rocked him to his core.

As he lay there with Ellie in his arms, his bare skin pressed against hers, he allowed himself to think of all the things he'd banished to the deepest recesses of his heart long ago—things like being a part of a family, holding his own child, committing to be with them no matter what happened in their future. Family was forever.

The day his mother had left, he'd vowed to never be vulnerable to love again. And yet the woman in his arms made him wonder if he could take that chance, no matter the consequences.

◆ ◆ ◆

Ellie came awake with someone tracing slow, scorching circles around her breasts. She opened her eyes and looked up into Connor's bright-green gaze.

"Morning, sunshine."

Her heart pounded not only at his touch but at the warmth in his voice. He dipped his head and kissed the side of her neck below her ear. He nibbled her neck, her chin, until his lips found hers.

When he drew back for a breath, she asked, "Should we be doing this now?"

"It's Saturday morning. There'll be no workers today." He pushed his thigh between her legs, opening her.

Her cheeks flushed. Sex in the morning was something new for her. "My Birthday Project is today."

He smiled down at her as he drove his sheathed erection inside her moist folds. "What time?"

Passion flared, then burned. "One o'clock." She barely managed the words.

He drove inside her. "We've got all morning to play."

She wrapped her legs around his and savored each long stroke. "Is that what you're doing with me? Playing?"

She sensed him shudder. "You know what they say about work and play. Unless you'd rather get back to work . . ."

"No," she breathed as he filled her body and her senses with delight and mind-melting pleasure. "Play is just fine." She tightened around him, seeking to hold, to caress, to heighten his pleasure and her own.

He dragged in a huge, broken breath. And release swept him, then her. A cascade of pleasure broke over her, bright and sharp, and spread through her in a flood of sensation more intense than it had last night.

He stared down at her before he captured her lips for another scorching kiss. His tongue taunted and teased in a possessive way that left her breathless and wanting more.

When he pulled back, he asked, "What is it about you that I can't resist?"

Her heart skipped a beat. "Last night I would say it was my skin-tight costume."

"I'd say it's a lot more than your leather pants." Laughing, he kissed her nose, then got out of bed. She feasted on the sight of his bare backside as he made his way to the shower. "I'll warm the water. Come join me."

She remained in bed, reveling in the scent of him that clung to her skin for a few moments more. It made her feel as if she belonged to him, even though she knew she never would. Not in the way she wanted. Their agreement would allow for nothing more. And yet, in the back of her mind, she couldn't help but wonder what it would take to make him change his mind.

CHAPTER FOURTEEN

The last Saturday of every month, Ellie put her event-planning skills into action for Seattle's homeless community. Her Birthday Project brought children, their families, and anyone else who wanted to celebrate a child's birthday to Freeway Park. The park was a green oasis in the heart of the city. She'd chosen the location for accessibility to the many homeless shelters and camps in the city.

The afternoon sky was a mix of sunshine and clouds. Filtered sunlight limned the fall leaves still hanging from the trees in hues of brilliant red and gold. The park's many water features added a soothing cadence to the hum of I-5 traffic as it flowed below the park through the city.

Connor had come to help her carry all her party supplies from the truck they'd rented. As if thoughts of him had conjured him up, he came around a concrete pillar, carrying several bags. Ellie's heart swelled at the sight. If she'd thought him sexy last night clad in black, then he was heartbreakingly handsome today dressed in jeans and a green flannel shirt that brought out the color of his eyes.

"Where do you want these gifts?" he asked, looking slightly unsure of himself.

"I'll take them," she said, stepping forward to receive the bags. His hands brushed against hers. A shiver of awareness rippled through her before he turned and left, ready to bring back another load of goods.

Ellie made her way over to the party area. Between forty and fifty people joined her each month, including eight to ten kids whose birthdays had passed without much fanfare or notice. Today she would change all that for those born in October with gifts, cake, games, and gift cards for the families who needed extra help.

Thanks to Connor and the $500 he'd given her on the night they married, this celebration would be extra special.

"Where do you want the cake?" he asked, carrying the big sheet cake they'd picked up an hour ago from the Macrina Bakery at the Belltown Café. The bakery had donated the cake, as well as paper plates and utensils.

"Put it on the table under the rental tent," Ellie directed.

"This cake is huge," he said, watching her as he had all morning with warmth in his gaze, his mouth poised on the brink of a smile.

"All of it will be gone by the time this event is over."

He looked around at the empty park. "When will they arrive?"

"Give it ten minutes," she said, checking her watch, noting the time: 12:45 p.m. "There'll be a park full of people. In the meantime, can you help me hang this poster with the names of the birthday children on it?"

"No problem," Connor replied, taking the duct tape she offered and following her to the concrete wall nearest the cake. In no time at all, the decorations were ready.

It warmed her heart every month to see so many local businesses come together to help. Local restaurants donated fruit, coffee for the adults, and milk for the kids. Stores donated either gifts of clothing for the kids or money that would be used to purchase the things they needed.

Each birthday child would receive a new coat and a new pair of shoes. The younger kids would receive a toy, while the older ones would get a refurbished iPod Touch with a gift card, to help them feel they fit in with their peers who had cell phones and all kinds of other electronics that the homeless families lived without.

Ellie had used Connor's donation for the iPods this month, as well as the bags they'd made up earlier containing tangerines, granola bars, and packets of air-activated hand warmers.

"Why do you do this?" Connor asked as he set the last of the bags out on a rented table. "Is there something in your past I don't know about?"

She laughed. "I was never homeless, if that's what you're asking."

"Then why? It obviously takes a lot of your time and effort to get all these donations from the community."

Her laughter faded. "Kids like Kevin deserve to feel special. I still remember the look on his face as he sang to himself in that alley near Pike Place Market. It didn't take much to make his face shine with happiness. Every kid deserves that—one day a year when they're the star. Even for homeless kids, such a moment helps their self-esteem and gives them hope for a better future."

"None of it is permanent. They'll grow out of the clothes, and they might lose their gifts or have them stolen in the shelters."

"No one can take away their memories. Those will be theirs forever," Ellie said, her voice breaking with emotion. "The people who come today are hanging on to each other. Despite losing everything, they still have the one thing that matters—a family. That's all those individual families have at night when they break up to go to different shelters."

Something close to pain flashed in his eyes before it was gone. Ellie considered that unspoken emotion for a moment. "Did your family celebrate your birthday?"

"My mom left us on my birthday. Every year after that, it was too painful to celebrate."

Unable to fight her own emotions anymore, tears came to her eyes. "Do you know why she left?"

He looked at her then. "You mean, did she leave a note? No. I always assumed it was because she no longer loved us."

A deep-rooted sadness reflected in his eyes. She studied him, trying to imagine what he would have been like as a boy. Then her thoughts strayed, and she thought about what he'd be like as a father to his own child.

Her heart fluttered. "Connor, I—"

Her words were interrupted by the sound of happy voices and running feet. Exactly as she'd predicted, the central area of the park filled with children and their families and friends, as well as those who wanted either company or something to eat.

She was about to start the party when she turned to Connor. That haunted look had returned to his eyes. "What is it? What's wrong?"

He plunged a hand through his blond hair while she waited. He remained silent, simply studying her with an unsettling intensity.

"Connor?"

The moment spilled out, lengthening in an odd way that made her heart speed up. He reached out and grazed her cheek with his knuckles. "It's nothing that can't wait," he finally said, breaking the tension.

She felt suddenly as though they'd missed out on something special—a moment that might never come again. Ellie's eyes teared up once more, but she forced her emotions back. She needed to focus on the party, not the man who distracted her at every turn.

Jordan had stopped by to help. Grateful for another pair of hands, Ellie put her to work cutting and passing out the cake after they sang a birthday song to all eight of the children who'd had birthdays that month.

The rest of the afternoon passed in a blur. She'd received so many thank-yous from the adults and hugs from the kids that she'd lost count. Their happy faces made all her efforts worthwhile, and explained why she would use much of the money Viola had given her for her work at Grayson House to continue these parties into next year.

It was comforting to know she didn't need to worry about the Birthday Project anymore when there were so many other things to worry about—like the way Jordan's gaze narrowed on her. Ellie knew that look. It was the one Jordan got when she'd figured something out.

Ellie didn't have to remain in suspense for long as Jordan finished cleaning up the cake mess before coming to join her. She pitched in, helping separate the garbage from the recycling. Once that task was complete, they'd leave them in a designated place for the city to haul away.

"What's up between the two of you?" Jordan asked.

Ellie glanced back to where Connor was disassembling the rental tent before returning her gaze to her friend. "What are you talking about?"

Jordan crossed her arms. "You're upset about something."

A chill went over Ellie as she wondered if she could hide anything from Jordan. She and Olivia had always laughed about Jordan's perception. They'd called it a superpower that must have come down along with her Irish heritage. Now that this perception was turned on Ellie, it wasn't so funny. "Oh, that?" she tried to brush her off. "That was just me getting emotional over the kids."

"No, it's more than that."

Ellie concentrated on tying the trash bags. "You're imagining things."

"To me it looked like you were mourning for something you should have but don't." Jordan waited until Ellie looked up. "Why would a newly married woman gaze at her very own husband that way unless there's something wrong in the marriage?"

"I'm fine," Ellie whispered. "We're fine." It was happening already. They were sowing the seeds of their eventual breakup. She should have been happy, because she wanted to confide in her friend. But that couldn't happen. They had to maintain the illusion of a happy marriage for another four weeks. "Please trust me on this."

"Okay," Jordan groused. "But if that weepy look continues next time I see you, I'm going to dig deeper—understood?"

Ellie nodded, grateful that Jordan's interference was through for today.

Connor returned a few minutes later after packing the equipment back in the rental truck.

"Thanks for all your help," she told him.

"It was inspiring to see you in action." He lifted his hand and ran his finger down her jawline.

She knew he wanted to kiss her, and she was amazed at how much she wanted to kiss him. The air between them all but crackled with mutual desire and need.

Yet he continued to stare at her with dark, hungry eyes. Maybe he hesitated because of Jordan's nearness. Or was it something more?

When she was sure he would kiss her the way a husband kisses his wife, he disappointed her by pulling away. "I'll return the rental truck and supplies. After that I have an errand to run. I'll be home later."

She nodded and, with her heart pounding, watched him go.

Beside her, Jordan groaned. "There's that look again. Come on, Ellie. What's going on? He wanted to kiss you. That much was obvious to a stranger, yet he didn't. You wanted to kiss him, and yet you remained still. That's not normal behavior between two married people. So start talking."

"We aren't two normal married people."

Jordan frowned. "What's that supposed to mean?"

It was time to tell someone the truth. "I want to tell you something, but you have to promise this will stay between us. You can't even tell Olivia."

Jordan crossed her heart with her finger. "I promise."

"Connor and I ended up married by mistake, and we're staying together only until his grandmother improves enough to handle the news that we're getting a divorce."

Jordan shook her head. "You might have married by mistake, but that is definitely heat I saw passing between the two of you."

"That's just it. Connor and I have an agreement. Sex only. No commitments. Once we finish transforming Grayson House back to her original glory for the Holiday Street of Dreams, we're done."

"But you're not really done, are you?" Jordan laughed. "You talk about Grayson House like it's a labor of love, not a business project. And as for Connor . . . there's a lot more going on between you two than just sex, whether either of you wants to admit it or not."

Ellie frowned. "How do you know what I want?"

Jordan gave her a sad smile. "Because I've known you for thirteen years, and from what I see, you're not just fixing up a house with Connor—you're making a home."

Ellie shook her head, denying the truth. "I'm making the house livable and sprucing it up so it'll be the best old Victorian in the holiday show."

"Delusions of Ellie."

"What?" Ellie gave a nervous laugh.

Jordan crossed her arms over her chest. An all-knowing smile tugged at her lips. "You're falling in love with him."

Ellie stood in silence as the words echoed inside her. "What do you know about love?"

Jordan bristled. "I know it when I stare it straight in the eye. You love Connor."

Ellie drew in a breath. "No, you're wrong," she said, even though she knew the words were a lie. "I like him a lot. I'm obviously crazy enough to play along with his let's-be-married-for-Viola scheme."

"It's more than that," Jordan said in a determined tone.

"I used to love him."

Jordan rolled her eyes. "You still do."

The truth washed over her in a cold, cleansing sweep. "Oh heavens. You're right. I still love him. I think I always have." Finally admitting her feelings was not a joyous thing like she'd always imagined. There was a twist of pain. Connor had made his feelings clear from the beginning. There was no room in his life for her. He'd told her before that he was married to his job.

"Have you told Connor that you love him?" Jordan asked, pulling her back to the moment.

"No," she said with a soft sigh of regret. "And I'm not sure I should. There is no commitment between us except the house, and in four weeks even that will be over."

"Four weeks?" Jordan asked. "That's plenty of time."

"For what?"

"To make him fall in love with you." Jordan fixed Ellie with a look that dared her to argue.

It was Ellie's turn to roll her eyes. "You can't just make someone fall in love with you."

Jordan frowned. "That man is already halfway there. He just needs a little push. Do you want to do the pushing, or should I?"

Ellie gasped. "There will be no pushing from anyone. Understand? If that's what's supposed to happen between us, then it will happen."

"You believe in destiny now?" Jordan snorted.

"Hey." Ellie bristled with indignation. "There's no need to get testy."

"You and Connor will both be so much happier if you'd accept your true feelings and not try so hard to fight them."

"This coming from a healer who tries not to get emotionally attached to her patients," Ellie grumbled. "Aren't you fighting your true nature, too?"

Jordan smiled. "Perhaps you're right. You and I would both be happier if we stopped trying to hide what we truly are."

Ellie returned her friend's smile. "Now that is something about which we can both agree."

◆ ◆ ◆

Connor cursed himself for a fool with every step he took away from the downtown park and Ellie. He should have kissed her.

No, he'd done the right thing. Kissing her would have been a mistake, because with her, one kiss was never enough. He could feel himself growing closer to Ellie every day they spent together. Since they'd come back to Seattle, his thoughts had been shifting away from his job at the lab to the woman he wanted in his bed. And his work was suffering. He had to do something to help shift his focus back to his car.

Even as he walked away from the park, he couldn't resist looking back. Ellie stared after him with concern in her bright-brown eyes. His stomach tightened; then he turned a corner, and she disappeared from view. Immediately he felt the loss.

Connor walked faster. He and Ellie had been married only a week, and yet in one week's time, she'd turned his whole life upside down. He hated needing her so much. Hated the way she made him want to be a better man.

He'd given up on love and relationships long ago, preferring to live in a cocoon of safety where he could do his research until dawn if needed, never having to take another person's emotions into consideration, never having to risk being hurt again.

Connor opened the door of the rental truck and slid into the cab. Instead of starting the truck, he clenched the steering wheel in his hands. Closing his eyes, he pictured Ellie lying in his bed, coiled in the sheet, staring up at him with satisfaction. He could still feel her in his arms.

Fire pounded through his blood. He wanted more of the same. He wanted to make love to her every night. To have her touch him, hold him.

But that wasn't part of their plan.

His heart heavy, he started the truck. The engine zoomed to life. Putting it in gear, he drove away from the park, from Ellie, from a life he would never have.

He'd been working on his prototype for the past nine years. The only way to be a success was to be the first to market. He could achieve that goal if he just stayed the original course he'd established between himself and Ellie. To make certain that happened, he'd arranged for a lawyer to meet him at the lab.

Connor had told Ellie in Las Vegas he'd take care of the divorce. It was time to start preparations for that eventual parting. The paperwork would take time to draw up; then they'd have to wait ninety days for the courts to finalize the divorce. If they started the process now, they'd be free of each other that much sooner and could return to their separate lives.

◆ ◆ ◆

Ellie started awake and glanced at the clock beside Connor's bed. Twelve thirty in the morning, and he still hadn't come home.

Home. She forced back a groan. Jordan was right. She'd been thinking of Grayson House as her and Connor's home. Restless, she got out of bed and wandered through the big, empty house. She weaved in and out of the rooms. In the family room, she found Zanzibar perched on the rounded crown of an antique chair, watching something outside.

She heard an odd sound—a strange whoosh, followed by a snap. Investigating, she made her way to the back door, opened it, and stepped outside.

There was no light from the new moon, but the stars were so bright she could see a shadowy figure on the back patio. Instead of fear, relief washed over her as she recognized Connor. Even in the half-light, she knew the contours of his face, his body.

He took the basketball in his hands and sent it flying toward the basket. It whooshed through the net. He twirled to catch it and froze at the sight of her. "What are you doing out here? Do you need something?"

I need you to come to bed and kiss me.

She swallowed. "I didn't know you were home."

"I couldn't sleep," he said, his tone guarded, distant as he turned back to his game, shooting the ball at the net once more.

He was pushing her away. "You're going to stay up until you go fishing with my dad at four o'clock then?"

He retrieved the ball, then froze. "That's today?"

"You committed to fishing, and I promised Viola I'd stop by and see her. It's not surprising neither of us can sleep."

Connor let out a slow breath. "That's less than four hours from now."

"You could cancel."

"No, I promised. If it's important to your father, it should be important to me." Connor swung around to face her, his features shuttered. "We should both get what little sleep we can."

"Or we could talk, because I know I won't sleep until we do. Will you?"

He hesitated a moment, then nodded his head. "Let's sit." He headed toward two wrought iron chairs that overlooked a rose garden. The late fall blooms glowed white beneath the light of the stars, and a pale, sweet scent twined through the night air.

They sat. "What do you want to talk about?" he asked.

She studied his face. There was no sign of his mood. He was hiding his feelings from her, and she wondered if there was any way to draw him out. "Why are you out here instead of in bed with me?"

"I just needed to think."

"About us?" she asked.

He brought his gaze to hers. "About our divorce."

Ellie's skin became hot and clammy at the same time. "What are you talking about? That's weeks away."

He stood and moved to a table near the corner of the house, where he picked up a white envelope that nearly glowed in the dark. He brought it to her and dropped it into her hands. "I made you a promise. We can file these divorce papers now if you'd like, since it takes ninety days for the divorce to go through. Look them over. Make sure you agree with everything. See if we need to change anything."

All the strength left her body. She collapsed back into her chair, sagging against the cushion. He wanted a divorce just when she'd realized she could never walk away from him.

Her body felt as if it were shutting down. It was all she could do to stop from curling in on herself.

He watched her now, as if waiting for a response, except she couldn't say anything. She'd entered that pain-filled place where speech was impossible. Fighting tears, she curled her fingers around the papers.

"Say something," he implored.

Ellie sucked in a breath at the loneliness in his voice and the pain in his eyes. "We agreed to stay together for at least five weeks. Or maybe," she added hopefully, "until Viola gets better."

"Once Grayson House is done and the holiday event opens, your work will be done. It will be time to move on."

A tear spilled onto her cheek as she continued to clutch the divorce papers. Silence stretched between them. How could she have been so wrong about what was happening? Finally giving in to a physical relationship with Connor had only made her crave more of the same. She wanted to argue with him, to try to convince him a divorce was a mistake. Then she remembered what he'd made clear from the start . . .

There will be no falling in love.

Too bad she hadn't heeded that warning sooner.

He'd also made it clear his self-driving car was his first priority. Did she really have a right to challenge that now when she'd always

---

come second to his work? "I need time to look over the papers," she finally said.

He nodded stiffly a moment before he turned and walked away.

He wanted a divorce.

It didn't matter that she wanted something more.

Reality returned. She'd put herself in this position by forgetting that this was all an act for Viola's sake. Viola would get better.

And Ellie's heart would never be the same.

Because as much as she tried to deny it, Jordan was right. She'd fallen in love with the man she'd married.

CHAPTER FIFTEEN

Death seemed imminent, and perhaps preferable to fishing with Ellie's dad on Sunday morning.

Not only had Connor been awake for the past twenty-five hours, but he could no longer feel his legs or his feet as he stood in the middle of the Skagit River in a pair of hip boots that did nothing to keep the freezing water out.

It was pitch-black, windy, and cold, and Connor tried to focus on something other than the current that tugged relentlessly at his body. One slip on a rock and his end would be swift. He'd been miserable before, but this experience was climbing the charts of the most miserable days ever.

Instead of being in hell, James Hawthorne stood in the river beside him, laughing. "Don't you love the rush of early-morning air slapping you in the face?"

"Yeah, it's awesome," Connor replied sarcastically.

James didn't seem to notice as he released yet another booming laugh. That laugh faded a few moments later as Ellie's father moved closer to him. "Son, other than fishing, I wanted to get you away from Ellie so we could talk man-to-man."

A chill that was not river induced trickled down Connor's spine. "About what?"

James cast his fly downstream. "Ellie's always been a cautious one. So why did she throw all that aside and marry you in Las Vegas?"

"You should be asking Ellie that."

Ellie's father turned away from his line. "Oh, I will, but I wanted to hear it from you, too. Why did she marry you in such a hurry after you broke her heart so thoroughly in high school?"

Happy he and Ellie had rehearsed their answers beforehand, he let them rattle off his tongue.

Accepting the answers, James tilted his head. "Then why not give her a honeymoon?"

That's what James was worried about, them not having a honeymoon? "We didn't have time for that. My grandmother had a heart attack, and we had to come back to Seattle to help her."

James nodded. "With her house?"

"That and other things." Connor kept his answers vague. He definitely needed to fill Ellie in on this conversation so they could sync their stories.

"You're not toying with her again, are you?"

"Never," Connor replied, even though he knew the word was a lie.

"Because if you do, I'll cut you into tiny pieces and feed you to the dog." James's features grew hard.

"You don't have a dog," Connor replied, his stomach turning.

"The fish then." James's face softened.

What could he say that James might believe now, and later when he and Ellie went their separate ways? "I only have Ellie's best interests at heart."

James studied him silently for a moment. "I believe you do," he said, his words no longer harsh. "That's why we trust you to do what's right for our little girl."

That sudden trust scared Connor more than anything the man had said or done. Something in James's tone told him he wasn't done yet. "What do you mean?"

"Julie and I talked last night. I haven't always been the father that Ellie deserved. I'd like to make up for that in some small way."

"How will you do that?" Connor asked.

"Her mother and I are sending you two on a honeymoon anywhere you want to go."

"A honeymoon trip for Ellie and me?"

"Talk it over with our girl. I'm sure she's gathered some ideas over the past few years. Since she didn't get her dream wedding, we thought we'd at least give her a dream honeymoon."

"Ellie really wanted a showcase wedding?" Connor asked.

James shrugged. "Who really knows what she wanted for herself? We'll never know now that the two of you ran off together instead. But she was very good at her job."

"She's still good at her job," Connor acknowledged, his chest tight as he remembered Ellie painting the walls, prepping for the decorating to come over the next few weeks.

"Glad you appreciate her many skills," James said as his line drew tight. He set the hook and started to draw yet another fish from the river.

While he and James talked, most of the other fishermen had moved downstream, claiming the noise was disturbing the fish. But James's booming voice didn't seem to bother the late-season river coho that bit at the man's trade-secret "pinkies."

James had already caught five fish in less than an hour. Instead of touting his success, he released each fish back into the wild, thanking the animal for a good time.

Connor had yet to catch a thing with the deadly hooks, except his own skin.

"Watch how you're casting there, son," James said with a rare frown. "Maybe you'll understand if I explain it in car terms, since you definitely understand cars."

Ellie's father held his fishing rod before him, loosening the line. "Your back cast is like starting the car. You can't drive if the car isn't started. The front cast is the journey. Let the line go, and the fly will do the rest."

Connor tried to whip the fishing line across the water, from back to front, but ended up catching the sharp hook on his head instead. "Not again," Connor groaned as pain zinged across his skull.

James laughed as he came to Connor's rescue. He plucked the hook from Connor's skin, inspected the fly, then tossed it back into the water, clearing the blood. "Use your forearm and a straight line, son, or my daughter might not like the bloody mess we bring home."

Concentrating, Connor tried to cast again. This time he slipped on a rock as he released the line. He caught himself, but couldn't hold back the rush of frigid water into his boots.

He sucked in a breath as shivers racked his spine. Ellie could be a bloody mess herself after her day alone with Viola. Perhaps the two of them could compare their wounds when they both returned home tonight.

If he returned home, Connor amended, in anything but a body bag.

◆ ◆ ◆

Right at noon, as requested, Ellie stepped off the hospital elevator and made her way to Viola's room. Outside the door she stopped. She heard men's voices coming from inside. She couldn't make out the words. Was Connor's father visiting? The two of them had met only briefly on the night they flew home from Las Vegas. Connor had made no effort in the past week to bring them together.

Putting on her best smile, she stepped into the room and gasped. She'd been expecting Clark Grayson, but four men stood like sentinels around Viola's bed.

In the middle of them, Viola sat up, smiling. A hint of a blush tinted her cheeks pink. She looked happy and much improved from a week ago.

Ellie knocked at the door before stepping inside. "Hello, Viola," she said cheerfully. "If you'd like me to come back—" Her words died as all four men turned her way. She didn't know them, and yet she did. Without their Elvis garb they looked like average seventy-year-old males. Yet they weren't.

"Allow me to introduce you to some old friends of mine," Viola said, her cheeks returning to their normal color. "This is Lenny, George, Ernie, and Aaron."

They looked different than they had in Las Vegas, definitely older without black wigs covering their balding heads. "You're the Elvises Connor and I met in Las Vegas." Cautiously, she approached and stopped beside Aaron. "How do you know Viola?"

Aaron turned to Viola with a question in his eyes.

Viola settled back against the elevated bed. "We used to have a singing act together in Las Vegas a long time ago."

Ellie's eyes went wide. "The dresses we found at Grayson House . . ."

Viola smiled. "You found those, did you? Those were the costumes I wore when we performed in all the best lounges back in the late 1950s."

"We were quite an act," Ernie added with a hesitant smile.

"We were quite an act, and so much more," Viola said without taking her gaze from Ellie's.

Viola turned to the man Ellie knew as Gold Elvis. "Ernie was the quiet backbone of our group. He might be shy, but he was also the optimist when things looked darkest."

George nodded. "That's the truth. Especially after you left us, Viola. Ernie was the glue that kept us together."

"I'm glad to hear that," she said, turning to White Elvis. "George was the lighthearted spirit of our little group."

"As opposed to my foul moods," Lenny countered.

Viola laughed at Red Elvis. "No, Lenny. You are the wise one. It was because of you that we got our start." Turning to Ellie, she said, "Lenny had connections in the industry that led to our first gig. Once we performed our first night, the rest was history."

"And what about me?" Blue Elvis asked.

Viola reached out and covered Aaron's hand with her own. "You were the unofficial guardian of our group. Your absolute devotion to your friends still shows in everything you say and do."

Ellie smiled at all four men. "It's nice to meet you all out of costume."

"Those days together were the best times of our lives," Lenny said wistfully.

"When we heard our girl was ill, we had to come see her," George explained. "It's not like we followed you back to Seattle or anything so that we could—"

"George!" Aaron interrupted. "What he means is that when we learned Viola was ill, we hopped the next flight out." He shrugged. "It was the same flight you and Connor took."

Ellie arched a brow. "It *was* you at The Lucky Club earlier this week."

Color flooded George's cheeks as he pressed his lips together, as though forcibly holding back a response. Ernie and Lenny looked away.

"We've been seeing the sights. Nothing more," Aaron said.

Ellie's gaze passed over each of the men positioned like sentinels around Viola's bed. They appeared quite fond of the older woman. At the realization that Viola and the Elvises had a connection, Ellie's thoughts drifted back to Las Vegas. Had she and Connor truly met by chance? Or was Ellie being far too suspicious for her own good?

As if sensing the direction of her thoughts, Aaron hurriedly turned back to Viola. "We should let you spend time with Ellie."

Viola nodded. "My new granddaughter and I have much to discuss."

"Bye, sugar," Aaron said, fluttering his fingers at her.

"We'll check in on you later," Lenny said, reluctantly leaving Viola's side as the others made their way to the door.

When they were gone, Viola straightened, as though tossing off the sentiment they'd brought out in her. "Have a seat, my dear. There are many things that need to be said." Her regal tone was back.

"You're looking well," Ellie said, ignoring the tone as she took a chair and moved it closer to Viola. "Are you feeling better?"

"As good as I can be after two heart attacks. But that is neither here nor there. You and I have a few things to settle. Let's start with the house."

Ellie sat back. What could Viola demand of them now? "What did you want to discuss?"

"My people tell me things are progressing with the exterior of the house and the interior painting, but you haven't done any actual design work yet. Should I be worried?" Viola gave her a penetrating stare.

Ellie drew an easier breath. She'd dealt with worried clients before. Viola was only one more. "Everything is on target. We needed to get the basics done first. It's like frosting a cake. You need the base coating of frosting before you can add any decoration."

"Grayson House is a cake now?"

"No, your house is not a cake. I was merely making the analogy that if we didn't fix the dry rot, broken windows, leaking roof, and other disrepair, no one would see the decorations, only the sad shape of the house." Refusing to let Viola rattle her confidence, Ellie stood. "You trusted me enough to hire me, Viola. What's changed?"

"I'm simply keeping tabs on things."

"I don't blame you one bit. You're investing a lot of money into Grayson House. You don't really know me, and you probably haven't had time to check my references, but if you'd like to now, they're listed on my website."

Viola frowned. "I'm not sure things need to go that far."

"That's up to you." Ellie shrugged. "We still have four weeks to pull the refurbishment and decorating of Grayson House together. I know I can do this, but it's your house and your choice. Do I stay or am I fired?"

To her amazement, Viola smiled. "I knew you had spirit. I can see why Connor fell for you in such a rush."

"Was this some sort of test?" Ellie asked, slightly dazed by Viola's shift in her emotions.

Viola nodded. "You passed, if that's any consolation."

Ellie shook her head, trying to clear her confusion. "Did Connor know about this?"

Viola waved Ellie back to her seat. "Oh, no. He'd be upset if he knew."

Her frown deepening, Ellie sat. "Okay, so now that that's out of the way, what did you really want to talk to me about?"

"A wedding."

"Connor and I are already married," Ellie said, even as her heart jumped. Did Viola's people have something to report there as well?

The older woman's face lightened. "Not your wedding, dearie. Mine."

Ellie's jaw dropped. "To who?"

Viola smiled. "That's my little secret, but I'll give you a hint. He's one of the four men who left this room earlier."

Ellie was stunned. "Why tell me this and not Connor?"

"He'll know soon enough. We want to get married at Grayson House the day after Thanksgiving, with everyone there. That includes your family, as well as your and Connor's friends."

Still struggling with the whole concept, Ellie replied, "You want me to add planning a wedding on top of the Holiday Street of Dreams?"

"How much more work can it be? You'll already have the house decorated. We don't need anything special—maybe a cake, some flowers,

and if you'll choose one of the dresses in my closet for me to wear."
Viola's cheeks flushed pink, making her look ten years younger. "I'll
make it worth your while financially. You and Connor will have all the
money you need to start your new life."

Ellie's breath faltered. "Shouldn't you talk to Connor or your son
about all this?"

"Not them." Viola sighed. "I don't think Connor or Clark will be
too happy about me marrying again even though I lost my dear Spencer
over forty years ago."

"Connor told me your husband died after you were married for
thirteen years."

Viola nodded. "I had a perfect marriage. To think I deserve that
twice in one lifetime will not go over so well with my son or grandson.
But I can count on you, Ellie. You believe in true love. I can see it in
your eyes every time you look at Connor."

The older woman turned to her bedside and retrieved a small
wooden box. "It's because of that love that I wanted you to have this."
She placed the box in Ellie's hands.

Ellie snapped the hinged lid open to reveal a silver necklace with
filigreed edges that circled a large aquamarine stone. "It's beautiful,
Viola, but I can't accept this."

"The pendant is a family heirloom. The stone was mined in the
Cairngorms in Scotland, and handed down through five generations
of Graysons."

"No." Ellie handed the heirloom back. "It should stay with you."

Viola crossed her arms over her chest, refusing to take the heirloom
back. "You are Connor's wife and the future of this family. What better
person to keep the tradition alive but you?"

Left holding the box, Ellie curled her fingers around the wood. She
would accept the gift for now even though she'd never be able to keep
it, even if a small part of her wished otherwise.

A deep-seated ache settled in Ellie's chest. "I'll plan your wedding, Viola. But I won't accept any more money from you. You've already offered Connor and me a small fortune to refurbish the house."

Viola frowned. "I have more than enough to spare."

"No money or no deal."

"Agreed," Viola said, the word filled with capitulation.

Ellie had won that battle for now, but something else beat at the back of her brain. "Why get married now?"

Viola's face paled. "Because I'm in love."

"With which man?" Ellie asked, scooting closer as a thought occurred to her. Maybe this sudden marriage had less to do with any one of the Elvises and more to do with Viola herself. "Are you sure you should be getting married?" She and Connor were proof that even marriage didn't shield a person from feeling alone.

Fear flared in the older woman's eyes. "I'm dying."

"We're all dying, Viola."

"My heart could go at any minute," she whispered in a strained voice.

Ellie reached for Viola's small, withered hand. "You aren't alone. Connor and I are here for you for the rest of your life." Even as the words left her lips, Ellie cringed. Why was she making promises she couldn't keep?

Ellie felt like such a fraud. If Viola wanted to hold fast to a commitment to another human being in the last days of her life, who was she to convince her otherwise?

She'd found contentment with Connor again in only one week. If she died today, would she die happy?

Yes, the answer whispered across Ellie's heart.

Viola released a heavy breath. "I'm not worried about being alone. I know you and Connor will be there for me. It's just that I really do love him," she told her. "You know what love feels like . . ." Viola watched her expectantly. "I want more warmth, more security, and a little less uncertainty for my last days."

The weight of Viola's words settled on Ellie's shoulders. She did know that feeling. And she'd be lying if she didn't admit she wanted more of it in her life. "I'm sorry, Viola. I didn't mean to doubt your love. When will we get to know who the lucky man is?"

A radiant smile lit Viola's face. "As soon as I tell him."

CHAPTER SIXTEEN

"How did your day with Viola go? Was it as treacherous as mine?" Connor asked when Ellie came home. He didn't have the strength to get up from the couch in the family room, nor did he want to disturb the ice pack on his head or the one behind his neck.

Concern turned her face pale as she came to his side, kneeling on the floor beside him. "What happened to you?"

"Your dad tried to kill me."

"What?" She grabbed the ice pack from him and flinched at the wounds on his head. "Did you come across a bear?"

"No." Connor wished he had a better story to tell. "These are all self-inflicted wounds."

Ellie sat back and pressed her lips together, no doubt fighting a smile. "It was that bad?"

"Terrible. Your dad was very patient. Though the sixth or seventh time helping me get the fly out of my head, he wasn't as gentle as the first."

"Well, at least that's over. You did your duty as the new son-in-law. We'll be divorced before he can invite you to go fishing with him in the spring."

At her words, heaviness descended over him. For an insane moment, he considered fishing again if it kept Ellie in his life.

Any further thoughts died as the front door slammed open and footsteps sounded down the hallway. "Connor!" A moment later, his father appeared in the living room. His eyes snapped fire, and his jaw twitched. "What the hell is going on with Viola and your wife?"

Clark Grayson turned to Ellie, his six-foot frame towering over her. He looked like hell. His clothes were rumpled, and dark shadows were smudged beneath his eyes.

His injuries forgotten, Connor jumped off the couch and helped Ellie to her feet, standing beside her. "What's going on?" He'd never seen his father so fired up.

Suspicion clouded Clark's expression. "Ask *her*," he said, pointing his finger. He continued to swear under his breath.

Ellie's face was pale, but her chin was tipped up. She met his father's heated gaze with a spark in her own. "I can see that you're upset, and I'm sorry about that. I'm only doing what Viola asked of me."

"Which is?" Connor prompted.

"She wants to get married the day after Thanksgiving."

"To who?" Both men asked at the same time.

Ellie shrugged. "She's keeping it to herself for now, but she did say it was one of the Elvises."

Connor looked at her in surprise. "One of the Elvises? What are you talking about?"

"The men we met in Las Vegas. They're here in Seattle. I only learned this afternoon that those same men are friends of Viola's."

"Lenny, George, Aaron, and Ernie?" Clark Grayson scowled, and pain and confusion laced his voice. "The men she used to sing with? That was a lifetime ago."

"Looks like they've kept in touch," Connor replied, not knowing how else to respond. "And that one of them might have touched Grandmother's heart in a way no one has since Grandfather."

Clark's features darkened even more, his anger palpable. "I forbid such nonsense. We have to stop her."

"Why?" Connor asked, suddenly curious why his father was so upset at the prospect of Viola finding love again.

"The man will break her heart."

"How do you know that?" Ellie asked, her face turning speculative. "He might make her final days even happier."

Clark snorted. "I doubt that. More like a living hell. Marriage is for fools who believe in ideals that don't exist."

A week ago, Connor might have agreed. Now he wasn't so certain. But he'd never convince his father of that. His father was skeptical about things like love and forever. Mary Grayson had proved that giving your love to another could only end in disaster. And that's what Clark would continue to believe for the rest of his days.

"I don't know," Connor said. "Maybe . . ."

Getting nowhere with his son, Clark rounded on Ellie. "This is your fault. You put that idea into her head."

"Dad—"

Ellie stiffened. "I did nothing of the sort. Have you met Viola? No one can put anything into that hard head of hers that she doesn't want to be there. She's as stubborn as they come."

His father frowned, but Connor saw a light of understanding in his father's eyes. The man wasn't unaware of Viola's true nature.

Ellie's features softened. "Viola is Viola. Whether any of us like it or not, if she wants to get married, that's exactly what she'll do."

Clark's face hardened again. "Unacceptable. We have to do something."

"What are you worried about, Dad? Because this has to be more than Viola getting her heart broken. Are you worried about her will?"

"I don't want my mother's money. I want her to be happy."

Connor frowned. "What if getting married again makes her happy?"

"That's impossible," his father scoffed. "Don't you know by now that no Grayson can be happy when we put our trust in someone else? It's our destiny to be miserable and alone."

"That's not true," Ellie interjected. More gently she said, "We're all biologically inclined to be coupled for life."

Clark rolled his eyes. "Good grief. You really believe that?"

"Yes." Ellie stood her ground, her shoulders going back. "Haven't you ever heard the phrase 'Love makes the world go round'?"

"You're ridiculous—"

"Dad," Connor interrupted, "don't talk to her that way. Ellie can believe whatever she wants to. As for staying away from Viola, that's not going to happen. Ellie's my wife."

Some of the fire left his father's eyes as he shook his head. "Has my life taught you nothing?"

Ellie looked at Connor with uncertainty in her eyes, as though waiting for him to either agree with his father or defend their marriage. With his next heartbeat he knew his answer. He'd never do anything to hurt the woman who'd agreed to help him save his grandmother. "Your life and your mistakes are yours and Mom's. I deserve a chance to make my own, or not."

"But your grandmother could be hurt because of your wife's interference."

"Viola's an adult. She can make her own choices. And if Ellie wants to help Viola get married again at her own request, then I'll support them both."

"I'm trying to spare everyone eventual pain. Why won't you listen to me?" his father asked with a sigh.

"Because pain is sometimes the risk a person takes in order to experience the greatest of joys," Ellie said.

Clark set his jaw and turned to Connor. "You won't help me stop this foolishness?"

"No, I won't," Connor replied.

"Then I can't wait for the day I can say, 'I told you so.'" A moment later Clark stomped back down the hallway and slammed the door shut.

They stood there for a long moment, letting the silence surround them until Ellie finally said, "What just happened?"

"You finally got to meet my dad," Connor said with a self-deprecating laugh.

"That's what you had to grow up with?" she asked, her voice strained.

He nodded.

"Then it's no wonder why you don't trust people with your heart. You've been told all your life that women will only hurt you."

He wanted to argue, but her assumption was true. The women he'd trusted had only confirmed that truth—that no woman could ever love him fully. "Viola really wants to get married again?" he asked, changing the subject—a sign he wanted to steer the conversation from himself.

Ellie arched a brow. "Yes, and if that's what she wants, who are we to stop her?"

"No idea about the bridegroom?"

She shook her head. "I suspect we'll find out soon enough." Ellie then filled him in about meeting the other Elvises and about what Viola had told her about each one.

"She's in love with one of the Elvises?" Connor asked, surprised and a little baffled by these new men, or old men, who'd reappeared in his grandmother's life.

"Seems so," Ellie agreed.

"Viola is always full of surprises."

"She's not the only one . . . you surprised me when you defended me to your dad."

Connor shrugged, trying to keep things light.

She studied him as if she was trying to figure him out. "You do believe in love, don't you?"

He shrugged. "I don't know. I've seen little evidence that true love exists in my own friends and family." He paused. "Well, except maybe with Max and Olivia. But for most people it's an unattainable goal."

"You don't really believe that, do you?"

"What if I do?" he asked irritably.

When she reached for his hand, he dodged her touch.

Her face fell, and he knew he'd hurt her by pulling away. "No one knows what's in your heart but you, though your actions over the past week tell me a story that doesn't quite live up to your words."

"And what story is that?"

"That you care about me more than you're willing to admit."

Connor had no answer for her. All he could do was return her steady gaze, fighting the turmoil inside him as he stared at her full, moist lips.

She broke eye contact with him. "When you're ready to talk about that, you know where to find me." She scooped up his ice pack and placed it in his hands before walking away.

Blood pounded through his veins as he watched her go, as did a craving for her that was hard to deny. She'd awakened something in him that he'd tried to ignore for years. The need for a home. For family. For love.

Ellie deserved those things, but not with him. He would only bring her heartache and pain when he couldn't give her that part of himself he'd always kept hidden.

She could never be his.

When their agreement was over, she could go back to the family who loved her and to her old life, where she could find a man who would give her everything she needed to be happy.

He clenched his fists around the ice pack in his hands, as his heart suddenly hurt worse than his head.

The conversation with his father had thrown Connor off balance, bringing back memories of the first woman to hurt him—his mother.

Leaving Ellie behind, he stepped out the front door and headed down the street.

For the first time in a long while, Connor allowed his thoughts to turn to his mother without fighting the questions that were always there. What made a woman leave her husband and child? Had she been unhappy or unfulfilled? But how could that be, when every memory Connor had of his mother was of her smile, a true wrinkles-around-her-eyes, joy-reflecting-from-her-soul kind of smile?

He and his parents had spent every moment they could together: playing Frisbee in the backyard, taking long walks through the nearby park, and watching scary movies while huddled together as they tried to comfort each other during the really scary parts. His mother leaving behind what had seemed like a happy family had never made any sense to Connor, but he had accepted that she'd gone.

Connor suddenly understood that this was the difference between his father and himself. He had accepted his mother's absence in his life. His father had not. Instead, he'd allowed himself to be engulfed by pain and loss. Those emotions poisoned his every interaction with anyone he cared about. That was why he objected to Connor's marriage to Ellie. It was why he didn't want Viola to remarry. He didn't want his mother or son to have the same potential for pain.

Connor stopped walking at the realization. His father was afraid for them. But fear did not have to guide a person's life. Suddenly Connor wondered what his father's fear had prevented him from doing. Had his father tried to find Mary Grayson? Where was she now? Had she started a new family? Or was she as damaged and alone as Connor and Clark?

As the questions flooded his mind, Connor started walking again, changing his direction, heading toward the Twelfth Avenue police station. His friend Trevor, a detective with the Seattle Police Department, should be working. Trevor owed him more than one favor. Perhaps it was time to call one of those in.

Trevor was good at finding people who didn't want to be found.

It was a long shot, locating a woman who'd vanished from their lives more than twenty years ago. But suddenly it felt like the right thing to do. Only time and a little investigative work would reveal the truth.

CHAPTER SEVENTEEN

Two hours later, Connor returned home to find Ellie lying in bed awake. "I'm sorry, Ellie," he said. The words were raw. No longer angry and desperate for the comfort of her touch, Connor slipped into bed beside her.

Her response was a kiss that led to a long night of incredible sex.

The next morning when the sun filtered through the bedroom window, Connor woke first. Needing to head to work, he finally summoned the strength to pull out of Ellie's arms. He liked sharing a bed with her, liked their limbs damp and tangled after a night of lovemaking. He especially liked the way she looked in the aftermath—her expression serene, her hair a wild tumble, her skin aglow with warmth.

Last night her voice had drifted through the darkness. "It's so easy to forget about everything else when we're like this."

"So easy," he'd replied, knowing exactly what she referred to . . . the promise they'd made to stay uninvolved. Yet each night he spent in her arms brought him dangerously close to breaking their agreement. Part of him wanted to push her away, to keep his mental distance, and to put them back on more even ground that didn't involve thoughts of her lying in their bed with a banked fire in her eyes. The other part of him was losing his grip on the situation. He wanted her with a need that went well beyond reason, making thoughts of giving her up excruciating.

But he had to. The last ten days since they'd been married had proven to him that he couldn't split his attention between two masters. He'd tried to keep both Ellie and his development team happy, responding to each of their needs, without success.

He would have to choose.

Regardless of what his body wanted, the choice had already been made. There was no room in his life for Ellie, not when he was so close to finalizing the artificial intelligence he needed to push his self-driving car into a realm above the rest. All that remained were a few more hours of coding and testing, and he'd be done.

Lingering by the bedside, he looked down at the woman he cared about far more than he should. Her hair lay across her pillow in a tumbled mass. The featherlight weight had draped across his chest only moments before in a silken caress. With his next heartbeat, his decision faltered, replaced with the wish that they were two different people in a different life where they could be together.

Ellie would be fine on her own with Grayson House. Because of her organizational skills, the refurbishment and preparations for the house's showing were ahead of schedule. Most of the remaining tasks were design elements she had tucked away in that creative mind of hers.

When he'd asked her last night about going into the lab from now until Thanksgiving, she'd responded with a casual, "That's fine," as though she didn't care if he were gone, or she didn't need him any longer.

Connor turned away from the bed. He had to keep his focus on his work and nothing more. Quietly he dressed and headed out of the room. Morning sunshine lit his way down the staircase. At the top he paused at the sound of a cat hissing below.

"Zanzibar?" Connor called as he took the stairs two at a time. At the bottom, he flicked the lights on to find the cat on top of the grandfather clock, the door to the pendulum swung open, and the foyer and parlor trashed.

He reached up to the cat, and the nervous creature jumped willingly into his arms. He held the animal close, stroking his fur. "It's okay," he said, even as the back of his neck prickled. Was someone still in the house?

With one hand, he plucked the red roses from a metal vase that lay on its side on the hall table, a puddle of water languishing on the floor beneath, then picked up the vase. Gripping the makeshift weapon in his hand, he set Zanzibar down and headed silently down the hallway. In the kitchen, the cupboards and drawers hung open, everything inside them askew. The contents of the trash can littered the floor, as did the decorating supplies Ellie had left on the table. Greenery, flowers, and Christmas ornaments were everywhere, making the kitchen look as though Christmas had exploded within its walls.

With the crunch of broken ornaments beneath his feet, Connor moved through the living room, family room, and dining room to discover they hadn't been spared. The furnishings were turned on their sides and upside down. How had he and Ellie not heard anything during the night with this kind of destruction?

He growled as the answer came to him. It was because they'd been upstairs in bed and otherwise occupied.

"Who would do such a thing?" Ellie's voice came from behind him.

He turned around. At her wide-eyed stare, he lowered his weapon and set it on the ground. "I don't know. Judging by the kitchen, I'd say it's someone who doesn't want us to finish the house."

A soft meow came from Connor's feet. He bent and scratched the cat behind the ears while he studied Ellie. Confusion clouded her brown eyes.

"The decorations are ruined, but that doesn't mean we can't purchase more. If they were truly trying to stop us—" She gasped, turned, and raced for the foyer.

Before he caught up with her, she was out the front door. She jerked to a stop on the sidewalk, examining the exterior of the house in the pale morning light. "No damage," she said, her chest heaving. "Thank goodness, the house is fine."

"Then what was this all about?"

Seconds ticked past as they made their way back inside. "Does it look like anything is missing?"

Her gaze traveled over each room's contents as they wandered through them once more. "Nothing appears to be missing. Aside from antiques, Viola doesn't really have much of great value in the house."

Her voice hung in the air between them. *Great value?*

His research.

The thought stopped him in his tracks. His lab was secure. Maybe that was why someone had broken into his home instead. Not that he'd ever be such a fool as to leave such important work in an unsecure location.

A crash sounded from upstairs.

Connor raced up the stairs and toward the sound that had come from the master bedroom. Ellie followed in his wake. Inside the room, the paintings were askew and the furniture tipped over like below.

His heart pounded. He drew a breath, trying to keep his anger and frustration at bay. He needed a clear head to figure this all out.

"The robber was just up here." Ellie's breath hitched behind him. "And look—the window's open." Her eyes were wide, her face pale. She clutched her hands before her. Even so, he could see she was shaking.

With a growl of frustration, Connor moved to the window and threw the drapes completely aside in time to see a dark figure jump down from their six-foot fence and vanish from sight. He wanted to stay and comfort Ellie, who was visibly shaken, but he had to follow the intruder if they were ever going to have answers.

"Stay here," Connor ground out. He turned to go, but stopped when Ellie placed a hand on his arm.

"Be careful," she said, then released him.

He inclined his head to her. "Call the police."

"I will."

Without looking back, Connor tore after the intruder. He pounded down one street, then another, until only the echo of his own footfalls came to his ears. He'd lost him.

Just as he returned to Grayson House, the police arrived. Connor walked them inside. He found Ellie standing in the doorway with Zanzibar in her arms. He almost smiled at the sight of the two of them coming to terms with each other in a time of crisis.

"Any luck?" she asked.

He shook his head. "Whoever it was got away before I could get even a partial description. But the intruder must have been male judging by the height and build."

Over the next forty minutes, he and Ellie gave the police what information they could and promised to call if they found anything missing. When they were finally gone, Connor leaned against the door. "We're getting an alarm system today. I won't allow anything to happen to you, not when I can do something to avoid it."

She tried to smile, but her attempt was more like a grimace. He couldn't blame her. The break-in was frightening, to say the least. "What could they possibly want from us or this house?"

He didn't want to upset her any more, but she had to know they weren't after her or anything in the house. "I'd bet they were after my research, if not the prototype of my car itself."

"Is your car still here?" she asked, her voice pained as she placed a comforting hand on his arm.

"I didn't bring it home last night. It's safe and locked up at the lab."

"How can you be sure? Is there someone you can call?"

"I'll need to go in to the university and check."

"Then go."

He shook his head. "I want to be here for you. To help you set the house to rights."

"I can take care of that. I'll call Jordan and Olivia. They can help."

He patted her hand, then reluctantly removed it from his arm. "I'll call your dad. I'd feel better if you had a man here with you."

Ellie frowned and grabbed a tipped-over glass vase from the kitchen table. "I'm perfectly capable of defending myself."

One corner of his mouth quirked at the sight of her. She looked like a fierce warrior with that glass vase held up, poised to strike. "I have no doubts about your abilities to protect yourself or this house, but it would make me feel better knowing you weren't alone. Please? Let me call your dad."

"I'll call him," she said. "You get on your way to the lab."

He nodded and let go of her hand, instantly feeling its loss as he headed out the door. He knew he needed to make certain his research was safe, yet he had the insane urge to stay with Ellie at any cost.

Once he reached the University of Washington and his robotics lab, he hurried inside. Only two members of his team had arrived. After a quick inspection, Connor was pleased to see his prototype was safely locked away in the lab and his research was secure in the safe.

As a precaution, he placed a call to university security, requesting an on-site officer for the next few weeks. Until he could finish his work, he would need to protect it.

If only he could be in two places at once.

CHAPTER EIGHTEEN

Ellie spent the next three weeks in a blur of activity as she finished staging each room of Grayson House. Her vision was taking shape, even if Connor was no longer home during the day to help her. Ellie didn't mind his going into the lab each day; his absence made it far easier to concentrate on her job.

Then at night, she welcomed him in her arms, much to their mutual satisfaction and fulfillment. She could no longer imagine sleeping without Connor by her side. His lovemaking was as passionate as it was tender. She could feel caring in each stroke of his hand, each thrust of his body, though he never voiced those emotions. And yet he had written her that poem . . .

Perhaps those were the only words she'd get from him—simple words inked in pen. A sinking feeling settled over her. It was time for her to accept that this was all he was capable of, or she'd be the one who walked away from this experiment with a broken heart.

Turning her efforts toward something she controlled, she'd hired a team of professional designers to implement the decorations. This morning as she walked down the stairs, Ellie allowed herself a moment's pride. All their hard work had transformed the already-grand house into something truly magical. Two steps later, her delight faded. It was only three more days until the Holiday Street of Dreams and Viola's wedding. Ellie had accomplished almost everything she'd set out to do, which meant she'd soon be leaving Grayson House behind.

Viola had recovered enough to leave the hospital and return to her assisted-living residence. She still had a long way to go in her recovery, but the bloom of love in her cheeks and her heart seemed to give her the determination she needed for a full recovery before her wedding.

Ellie stopped at the bottom of the stairs. She turned back to look up at all they'd achieved. Greenery wrapped the banister of the grand staircase from the bottom to the top floor. White poinsettias, white ribbons, clear glass ornaments, and pinecones were the only decorations she'd used, allowing the house's natural beauty and charm to shine through.

A fifteen-foot tree welcomed visitors in the foyer, lit with LED candles that looked as if they'd come straight out of the Victorian age, along with the same decorations as the rest of the house.

Outside, she'd wrapped the house in white twinkle lights and cedar boughs at the first- and second-story rooflines. Wreaths with big red bows hung from every window along the front and back of the house, completing the storybook vision from an earlier age.

Connor had offered to help her with one of the more complex outside decorations. Since Lenny, George, Aaron, and Ernie were an accomplished singing group, she and Connor had hired them to dress in Victorian clothing and sing carols from long ago in a recording studio in the city. Connor's plan was to project their image in a 3-D hologram on the front lawn. She'd coordinated the songs and the costumes for the four men. Connor had said he would take care of the projection for both daytime and nighttime viewing.

Ellie turned and headed for the kitchen. It was time to get started on the last pieces of her design. In the three remaining days before the showing, she had to bake and decorate enough gingerbread houses to place in each room of the house.

An hour later, the familiar scent of cinnamon and cloves permeated the air in the kitchen as Ellie took gingerbread that would become the first houses out of the oven. As she set the gingerbread on racks to cool, a knock sounded at the door.

A quick glance at her watch let her know it would be the photojournalist from the *Seattle Gazette* who'd arranged to stop by and take pictures of Grayson House to advertise the Friday event.

After a tour and many pictures of the house, Ellie brought her guest back to the kitchen for a cup of tea and a gingerbread cookie made from the leftover dough.

"You pulled off a miracle, Mrs. Grayson. None of us at the paper thought you could manage it in the time you had," Rachel Gatis admitted, chewing on a warm cookie.

"It wasn't easy," Ellie said with a laugh as she took another sheet of gingerbread from the oven and placed it on a cooling rack.

"What's your secret?" Rachel asked.

"I had lots of help. If you'd like a list of the contractors who provided the services, I'd be happy to provide one."

"Readers love that," the photojournalist said as she sat back in her chair. "What's next for you? Had any new job offers during the renovation?"

Ellie inhaled the gingerbread-laden air. "I don't know. I hadn't thought that far ahead. Guess I'd better start worrying about another job sometime soon." By Friday she'd be right back where she'd started—with no clients . . . and no husband.

Rachel shrugged as she finished the last of her gingerbread and her tea. "I doubt you'll have to wait long for an offer once these photos run. You'll have them lining up for your interior-design skills. Want me to put the word out that you're looking for work?"

Ellie turned back to the gingerbread, rearranging the pieces on the cooling rack as though the cookies needed her attention. She would miss the event-planning part of her business if the only jobs she got from now on were for design. But at least she'd have work. Finally she nodded. "Anything you can do to help would be gratefully appreciated, Rachel. Thank you."

The photojournalist stood up, preparing to leave. "No, thank you for the preview and the treats. I'll get these photos online right away. They'll run in the print edition of the paper the day after Thanksgiving." Rachel turned to leave, then paused. "That was the best gingerbread I've ever eaten, by the way."

"It was my grandmother's recipe," Ellie replied. "I don't think she'd mind if I shared her recipe with others. Would you like a copy?"

"Absolutely."

Ellie saw Rachel out, then shut the door behind her, releasing a breath she hadn't realized she'd been holding. She turned to look at the grandfather clock and his ever-present frown. There was nothing magical about the face on the clock. The artist who'd painted the old man had done so in a way that when people looked at the face of the clock, they might see something different than the person standing next to them did. The painting was an optical illusion of sorts. Regardless of that knowledge, Ellie frowned at the old man's face, and the frown clearly etched there.

"I know. I'm a disappointment. You don't have to rub it in," Ellie groaned. Leaving Grayson House and Connor was the last thing she wanted to do, yet she might not have any other choice.

◆ ◆ ◆

After she'd spent the entire day baking and decorating gingerbread houses, Ellie was happy to escape to her Tuesday-night retreat at The Lucky Club with her friends. When she arrived, Jordan and Olivia were already there, drinks ordered and waiting.

Before Ellie said a word, she slipped into the empty chair beside Jordan and downed the entire glass of pink champagne before her.

"That bad?" Jordan asked with wide, curious eyes.

Ellie set her empty glass down, then sank back against the chair. "It's time I tell you both the truth."

Jordan, already knowing part of what she planned to reveal, gave her an encouraging look.

Olivia frowned. "The truth about what?"

Ellie slowly straightened and brought up her chin. Telling her two best friends everything might help her find the peace she'd been searching for. "Connor and I might be married, but we're only staying so to give Viola something to live for."

"Oh my." Olivia blinked in surprise but rallied quickly. "So you're pretending to be married?"

"No, we're really married, but instead of getting an instant divorce like I wanted to in Las Vegas, Connor talked me into staying married until Viola's health improved enough to tell her the truth."

Jordan frowned. "Who decides when Viola is well enough?"

"We decided to end our marriage when Grayson House was finished and the Holiday Street of Dreams began. We figured that Viola would be better by then."

"What happens after that? You simply go your separate ways?" Olivia asked with a frown.

"Connor's already seen to our divorce papers. We'll have to wait until the usual waiting period passes, but then everything will be over between us." Ellie looked down at her clutched hands. "Only three more days until I'm unemployed and a soon-to-be divorcée."

Jordan scooted her drink over to Ellie. "I'm sorry things have to end this way."

"They don't." Olivia sat back against her chair with a mutinous look on her face. "You can't go through with the divorce. I've seen the way you two look at each other. It would be wrong to break apart what is truly meant to be."

"That's where you're wrong, Olivia. Our marriage was never meant to be. Connor has always and will always put his work above everything else—and that includes me." Ellie swallowed past the lump in her throat.

Olivia reached for her hand, and Jordan put hers on top of the others. Finally Olivia spoke. "I've never known you to be a quitter, Ellie. Let's figure out a solution to this problem. We're three smart women. I'm sure we can come up with something."

"I don't want to come up with any scheme. For once in my life, I'm being a realist. Connor made it very clear from the beginning what our relationship would and wouldn't become. I'm the one who changed. He didn't. There's nothing keeping us together."

Olivia smiled. "I wouldn't say nothing. You definitely have chemistry on your side."

Ellie blushed. "Even that's not enough. Great sex won't solve anyone's problems."

"I'd like to give it a try," Jordan said wistfully.

Ellie couldn't help but laugh. "Never fear, Jordan. With Olivia and I having already bungled our love lives, I'd say your turn is next."

"Hey," Olivia protested, hugging the tiny mound of her abdomen, "my relationship with Max turned out okay."

Ellie instantly sobered. "You are one of the lucky ones."

"We're all lucky," Olivia objected. "After all, isn't that why we started this get-together at The Lucky Club in the first place, because we were tired of being unlucky in love?" Olivia's voice broke on the last words, and tears filled her eyes. "Sorry," she said, dabbing at her eyes with her napkin. "It's the hormones. Everything emotional makes me cry these days."

Jordan and Ellie shared a glance before nodding. Neither of them felt too lucky at the moment, but neither of them would argue with their friend. If she wanted to believe their weekly meetings had changed the course of their lives, who were they to argue with a hormonal, pregnant woman?

Desperate to change the subject, Ellie said, "Do you have plans for Thanksgiving?"

Jordan scooted her drink back and took a long sip, presumably to avoid the subject.

"Max and I are hosting a dinner for both of our families. Paige and the Millers and all their foster kids are coming, too," Olivia said.

"That sounds like a lot of work for you," Ellie replied.

"Not at all." Olivia's eyes dried and her smile returned as the hormones settled back into a more normal state. "Max hired a chef. He won't let me do a thing until the baby's born."

"That's in five more months." Jordan's eyes went wide.

Olivia shrugged. "He's being overprotective, I agree. When I need to, I'll resurrect my stubborn streak."

Ellie turned to Jordan. "What about you? Please say you'll come. I could use some support."

Jordan frowned. "Isn't Viola getting married the same day?"

Ellie nodded. "To her bridegroom, whoever that may be."

Jordan raised a brow. "Has she told the guy he's getting married yet?"

Ellie winced. "Since they needed to apply for a wedding license, I sure hope so. But she's keeping the details a secret."

Jordan threw Ellie a conspiratorial wink. "We could go to the courthouse and search the public records."

Ellie laughed. "And give Viola a reason to make my life a living hell? No, thank you!"

"I'm not working . . . all right. I'll come. The day will be entertaining if nothing else," Jordan agreed.

"So glad I can provide you with a distraction," Ellie said, smiling at the one person who could help her keep her emotions in check during one of her last few days with Connor.

◆ ◆ ◆

Since Ellie was out for the evening with her girlfriends, Connor decided to do something he'd been dreading for the last three weeks: seeing his father. No matter how painful facing the truth might be, neither of them could avoid it any longer.

Connor headed to his father's Queen Anne home only a few miles away from Viola's. Parking his car in the driveway, he allowed himself a nostalgic smile at the sight of the garage. It was the place where many of his initial inventions had occurred.

The kitchen light and living-room lights were on, signaling his father was home. He climbed the shallow front steps and knocked on the door.

His father answered the door with a puzzled look on his face. "What brings you around?" he asked as he stepped aside and allowed Connor to enter. "I thought you'd be at home with that wife of yours. Enjoy it while it lasts."

Biting back a retort, Connor replied instead, "I came to see how you are and to give you some news."

His father's sharp hazel eyes met his, but he remained silent as he took a seat in the living room in his favorite recliner, the one he'd had as far back as Connor could remember. That was his father in a nutshell: a man who held on to things—not people—as long as he could. With hope, tonight he would let go of his past once and for all.

"We need to talk about Mom."

"No." His father scowled. "I asked you never to mention that woman in my presence a long time ago."

"Don't you think it's been long enough? Harboring hate has ruined not only your life but mine as well," Connor went on, undeterred. They would have this discussion whether his father liked it or not.

His father's gaze grew increasingly sharp. "If that's what you want to talk about, you can leave." The bitterness in his voice was no surprise.

"She's dead."

Clark Grayson's stormy expression faded, leaving his face pale and gaunt. There was a long pause before his father swallowed and asked, "How do you know this?"

"My friend Trevor ran her information through the SPD database. I figured twenty-four years was long enough for us to not have any answers." They'd come this far; there was no retreat now.

His father closed his eyes and nodded. "Okay, so she's dead. I guess I can stop worrying about running into her someday and not knowing how to respond."

"There's more."

His father snapped his eyes open. He regarded Connor with reluctant curiosity. "Well, don't keep it to yourself. You got me this worked up. You might as well go all the way."

"She died six months after she left us."

Clark clutched his hands in his lap.

"Trevor found the hospice center where Mom died, and I spoke to her hospice nurse. Even after all this time, the woman remembered Mom because of the way she talked about her husband and son."

"She had regrets?" his father asked in a raw voice.

Connor nodded. "The nurse said Mom's last words were all about how she wished she could have watched her son grow up, and how deeply she regretted not being able to grow old with her husband at her side."

While his father stared off into the distance, Connor said, "Mom died from an inoperable brain tumor."

His dad remained silent for a long moment, but emotion definitely stewed behind his hazel eyes. "Not sure what you think this all proves."

"It proves," Connor continued, determined not to let his father dismiss what he said, "that she was sick before she left us, though neither of us knew. It also proves that it wasn't something we said or did or didn't do that caused her to leave."

Clark clenched his hands in his lap, his fingertips turning white. A sheen of tears came to his eyes. "She didn't love us enough to stay."

Connor shook his head. "I don't believe that. Not after talking to the hospice nurse. I believe she thought she was protecting us in some way by keeping us from her disease."

"I would've been there for her to the end. Watching her die would've been hard, but I could've done it." Tears fell onto his father's cheeks, and he sank back into his chair. "It would have been so much easier to actually grieve for her instead of harboring such hate for the majority of my life."

Connor knew how his father felt in that moment where truth collided with past beliefs. But only once his father faced the truth would there be space in his heart for possibility.

"We aren't hopeless, Dad," Connor said, voicing his newfound belief. "And it's not too late for both of us to find some happiness in this life."

His father nodded absently.

A moment ticked past, then another, until his father finally dragged in a huge breath. "Thank you for telling me and for being brave enough to find out what happened. I have a lot of thinking to do and some apologies to make." He eyed Connor approvingly, then looked down at his hands. He unfurled them, smoothing them on the legs of his pants. "I should have had the courage years ago to do what you did."

Connor held his father's gaze. "It doesn't matter who did what, when. What matters is what we do with the truth. And, if you'd like to hear about Mom yourself from the hospice nurse, she's agreed to talk with you."

"I'll think about it."

A heavy silence pervaded the room as both Connor and his father were caught up in their own thoughts. After a long while, Clark sat up. "Will you stay for dinner? I'd really like to spend more time with my son."

Connor offered his dad a smile. "Sounds great. What are we having?"

"Steak and beer sound good? I think a little celebration is in order."

"A celebration?" Connor asked, slightly perplexed. What could they be celebrating when he'd just told his father about his mother's death?

The muscles at the corner of his father's mouth pulled up in a funny way, no doubt because the man hadn't allowed himself a moment's happiness in years. "It's time we celebrated every one of those birthdays you missed. And it's time I started being the father you deserve."

"I love you, Dad."

"I love you, son." The smile he'd been trying to muster pushed its way forward, lighting his father's face in a way that made him look ten years younger, changing everything.

A sense of satisfaction settled over Connor, leaving him feeling energized, because the impossible suddenly seemed possible. Love had transformed his father. Could it do the same for him?

CHAPTER NINETEEN

Wednesday afternoon Ellie arrived home after running to the grocery store for two last-minute items she needed for their Thanksgiving meal. She found Connor waiting for her in the parlor with a thick manila envelope in his hands.

His full attention was on her the moment she stepped into the room. "Can we talk?" Connor's tone was warm and friendly, but something heavier reflected in his clear, green eyes.

She set her grocery bag down. "Sure. About what?" But she already knew.

"Tomorrow's Thanksgiving."

Ellie sat gingerly on the edge of the chair beside him. The way he looked at her, with that rather sad smile, sent a shard of fear to her core. This was it. He would hand her their final divorce papers, and the process would begin. Then after the ninety-day waiting period was through, their uncontested divorce would be final.

It was time for her to wake up from her dreamworld now, because he'd always said their agreement had an end date.

"Ellie? You look like you're a million miles away," he said.

"Sorry, just thinking. What were you saying?" She had to force herself not to lean toward him. No matter what he held in his hands, her attraction to him remained unchanged.

Connor shifted in his chair. "Our marriage—"

The words had barely left Connor's lips when his cell phone chimed. With a dark frown, he set the papers on the table beside him and drew his phone from his pocket. He glanced at the screen. "It's the lab. Sorry, I need to take this."

Her mouth felt dry, and her throat swelled. This was like that moment when the jury came back into the courtroom and was asked to render their verdict. The moments ticked past, fate suspended.

Connor continued to stare at her. His eyes clouded with confusion while he listened to the person on the other end of the line. "You're sure?" he said as the look in his eyes shifted to panic.

Her ragged heartbeat almost obliterated all other sounds.

"I'm on my way." He ended the call and stood, stuffing his cell phone back inside the pocket of his jeans. "I'm sorry, Ellie. This has to wait. There's been a break-in at the lab. It looks serious. I have to go."

"Of course." She stood.

Connor moved forward, his gaze fixed on Ellie's face. "We're not done here. We have so much more to discuss, if fate will only allow us." An odd grin came to his face.

The look did funny things to her brain and filled her with a renewed sense of hope. Or was she simply imagining things? She shook the thoughts away. "How did the intruder get past the security system?"

"No one seems to know. I'll be back as soon as I can." He leaned forward and pressed a kiss to her lips. It was over before it began, but the effect on her nerves was just as powerful as if he'd ravished her.

He grabbed his coat and left.

Ellie stood frozen as her gaze shifted to the white envelope Connor had abandoned. There was a note paper-clipped to the front. She moved closer to read what it said.

Do we have other options?
Connor

The cursive handwriting was neat and tidy. Exactly the kind of writing she'd expected of him. Smiling, she folded the note and put it in the pocket of her jeans. She could think of lots of options.

A moment passed, and her smile slipped. She should be thinking about the break-in and hoping there was a happy resolution there. Instead, she was breathing too fast and hoping with all her heart for the impossible to happen for Connor and her.

Had he decided to change the terms of their agreement? Maybe believing in happy endings wasn't going to break her heart in two. Perhaps she and Connor really could have the perfect future she'd imagined in her dreams.

While she waited for him to return, she had another happy ending to facilitate. After putting the groceries away, she made her way up the grand staircase to the ballroom on the second floor.

She'd turned the wide-open space into a winter wonderland where Viola's wedding would take place. Flocked Christmas trees decorated with crystals and white lights lined the perimeter of the room. She'd set the white chairs, white runner, and two rows of white poinsettias situated around four towers of white flowers that lined the approach to the white wedding bower. Two rows of pillar candles in clear vases would give the room a magical, fairylike feel when lit.

For Viola, she'd chosen a beautiful ice-blue satin gown encrusted with seed pearls. Viola had assured Ellie the groom would wear white. Did that mean her bridegroom would be George in his White Elvis costume? Those Elvises who were not the groom would make up the rest of the wedding party.

At the thought, Ellie frowned. It seemed rather ironic that she and Connor, as well as Viola and her bridegroom, had started their marriages the same way—with the Elvises involved. *Or was it a coincidence?* she wondered for the second time.

Connor had called it fate a short time ago.

Another realization crystallized, and she reached in her pocket for the note Connor had left her—a note in his handwriting. She studied the writing that was so different from the bold, almost slanted script on the notes and the poem he'd left before.

Suspicion sluiced through her, twisting her stomach. Someone else had written the other notes—someone else who desperately wanted them to stay together. The question was, who?

Had it been the Elvises who'd married them? Had she and Connor fallen into some twisted Elvis plot for Viola's sake? Had Viola manipulated everything that had happened between them?

Did Connor know? Maybe that's what he'd wanted to talk to her about, "their options." Not their divorce, but how manipulated the past five weeks had been for both of them.

Oh heavens . . . Ellie released a fractured breath as she staggered to the closest white chair. She dropped onto the seat, her legs suddenly numb.

Had any of it been real?

Viola's heart attacks had been real. Her surgery and hospital stay were proof enough of that. Ellie had to give the older woman credit for her perfect timing.

The sex had been real.

Ellie allowed herself a smile at the memory of Connor's kiss downstairs. Not even Viola could fabricate the spark that ignited between her and Connor with a look, a touch, or a kiss. Their mutual attraction was real, but was it enough to keep them together when the truth of Viola's deception came out?

A sound came at the door to the ballroom, interrupting her thoughts. Ellie spun toward the sound. "Connor, you're right. We need to talk."

It wasn't Connor who stood in the doorway. It was Amanda Frost.

"How did you get in here?"

Amanda's smile turned sinister. "Your husband left in such a hurry he forgot to set the alarm."

Comprehension dawned over Ellie. "That was you who broke into the lab?"

"No. Just a distraction in order to get what I really wanted."

She stepped slowly forward with her hand in the pocket of her dark coat—a dark coat that looked very similar to the one Ellie had seen on the person jumping over the fence after the house break-in.

"I want you to leave."

Amanda's face tightened. "We don't always get what we want."

Ellie stood, knocking her chair over in the process. She desperately tried to think of what to do, how she could take control of this situation. The longer she kept Amanda talking, the more chance she had of Connor returning home. "What can you possibly hope to accomplish by threatening me?"

Connor's ex-girlfriend stopped before her. "It's not you I want."

"Then what?"

She sucked in a breath, then in a controlled voice replied, "Your husband's research and his prototype. I figure if I take the thing he loves most, he'll hand it over willingly."

Ellie couldn't help it. She laughed. "That was a big assumption on your part."

Amanda frowned. "Why is that?"

"Because he'll never trade me for his research or his car. You might as well end whatever this is now before you're looking at more serious charges than breaking and entering. Twice."

Amanda murmured close to her ear, "I'm sure you underestimate yourself . . ."

A chill slid through her as Amanda's fingers clamped around her elbow.

Ellie swung her other arm, connecting with Amanda's chin.

She lurched back but only tightened her grip on Ellie's arm. *Damn, the woman is strong!* But if Amanda meant to take her somewhere, Ellie wasn't going to make it easy. She kicked Amanda's knee and wrestled out of her grasp. With her heart in her throat, Ellie raced for the door. She had finally found a purpose for the handcuffs Jordan had given her, except they were upstairs in her room.

Ellie had scarcely cleared the door frame of the ballroom when Amanda caught up to her. Ellie felt a sharp pinprick bite into her neck.

Her body went limp, and she watched Amanda smile. A heartbeat later, Ellie melted to the ground. Her last thought before darkness engulfed her was of Connor and how much she would miss him when she never saw him again.

CHAPTER TWENTY

Ellie's eyelids fluttered open. Too heavy to hold them in that position, she let them drift closed. It had all been a dream . . . a dream that smelled like dead fish.

Ellie forced her eyes open and found herself in a dark room. She could see nothing that gave her any clue to her whereabouts. There was a concrete floor beneath her. The air was cool, but not as cool as outside.

A wave of nausea rolled over her. The drug Amanda had given her was slowly wearing off, but not fast enough. With a groan, she rolled onto her side. It was then she realized her hands and feet were tied. Not wanting the fish smell to make her nausea worse, she took shallow, even breaths in an effort to clear her head.

Once the nausea was under control, she remained still and listened. When nothing came to her, she squeezed her eyes shut and focused, trying to make her addled brain work. Gulls squawked overhead. There was a sound of water as it slapped against wooden pylons.

The Seattle waterfront. If she put those clues together with the fish smell, then she could be nowhere else but at a fish-processing factory. There were several along Alaskan Way where someone could be held unnoticed for a long period of time.

A more terrifying thought occurred to her—was she simply here waiting for Amanda to put her on a boat? A boat made sense. It would be so easy to dispose of her body in the depths of Puget Sound once Connor refused her captor's demands.

Ellie drew a deep, steadying breath. Her new goal for the evening: avoid being killed.

If death did find her, she had only one regret—that she hadn't taken the chance to be honest with Connor and tell him what was in her heart. Because she knew he was the one for her.

Silently, in case Amanda was near, she tested the knots that bound her by straightening her legs. They were tied tightly together, making it impossible for her to walk. Her hands were tied tightly together in front of her. As her eyes adjusted to the darkness, she could see the hazy outline of the knot at her hands, and she smiled.

Obviously Amanda hadn't been a Girl Scout. She'd tied the rope together in the center of Ellie's hands with a figure-eight knot instead of a square knot. She could get out of her bindings in time.

Ellie brought her hands to her mouth and started working the knot loose with her teeth. The fact that she could do something to help herself, and hopefully ruin Amanda's plans, gave her courage—however false it might be. But at least she was doing something besides waiting to be fish bait.

A sound grated in the distance. "I hope you're not too groggy," a female voice said from the darkness.

Ellie stopped her gnawing, praying that if she couldn't see Amanda, Amanda couldn't see her. And if Amanda couldn't see her, maybe Ellie could rattle her. "Connor told me you were smart. But obviously not smart enough to find a way to abduct me without using sedatives."

A lantern flared on her left, flooding the room with pale, golden light. Amanda strode toward her until she stood above Ellie, her face expressionless. "Keep insulting me, Ellie, and something might happen to you before I can return you to Connor."

Ellie looked around her. She was definitely in a warehouse, one with high windows all along the side and a door on the far end to her left.

Too high for her to climb up to and escape. "Where am I?" she asked, not really expecting Amanda to reveal anything useful.

"Haven't you guessed?"

"A warehouse along Alaskan Way."

"You're very good at this game." Amanda smiled. "Want to play another game?"

"Such as?"

"Guess how long it'll be before that husband of yours notices you're gone?" Her smile turned cruel.

"I already told you—he won't care."

Amanda pulled a knife from her pocket, and the blade clicked open.

Ellie tried to keep her expression from revealing the terror that skittered across her nerves.

Amanda bent down and stroked the side of her cheek with the ice-cold blade. She lifted strands of Ellie's hair and hacked off a hunk.

Ellie flinched but held back a gasp.

"He'll care when I deliver this to him along with my demands."

Ellie swallowed roughly as the overwhelming scent of fish merged with her own fear. "What are you after, Amanda? Why do you want Connor's research so badly?"

Amanda's smile faded. "I'll get billions of dollars for all the technology his car will reveal."

"And a prison sentence."

Amanda shook her head as she stood, sending her long, dark hair cascading about her shoulders. The woman looked more like a super-model than she did a supervillain. But it would be wise not to underestimate her. "I'll be long gone to some foreign country before the officials realize what I've done."

That Amanda was telling her all this didn't make her own prospects for survival look great. Despite a shiver that racked her, Ellie continued with her questions. "Why couldn't you simply do the research yourself instead of stealing from Connor? First in college, now this? Don't you have any morals?"

"I'll let that insult pass. Why not? I'm feeling generous. I'll soon have all the money I could ever want." Amanda turned off the lantern, pitching the room into darkness once more.

"What a way to start your new life, as a thief and a murderer."

"I'm not going to kill you. At least not right away. That wouldn't be very exciting. Besides, I still have faith that your husband will come around to seeing our demands. I mean, why love a car when you can love a woman instead?"

Ellie drew a steadying breath, trying not to let Amanda's words undermine what little bravery she still possessed. She had faith in Connor as well, but when it came to his car, he was unpredictable. She'd had to compete for his attention from the moment they married.

Amanda moved away from her, toward the doorway off to her left. The metal door screeched open, then closed.

Ellie's heart fell at the sound of a dead bolt sliding into place.

Instantly she brought her hands back up and, doubling her efforts, chewed at the knot, all the while cursing Amanda for the darkness.

A shiver went through Ellie, but she forced her fear away. Instead of allowing the darkness to close in around her, she closed her eyes and imagined the ballroom and all the thousands of twinkle lights she'd woven into the trees and around the room.

Viola and mystery Elvis's wedding was not one she intended to miss.

◆ ◆ ◆

When Connor arrived at the lab, his project lead was waiting for him at the door. In the distance Connor could see two medics near his office, moving someone to a gurney. A pool of blood darkened the concrete floor. "Who's hurt?" Connor's brain fired in all directions as he took in the scene.

"Alex Ferrara. I found him sprawled on the floor. Someone bashed him in the head," Mike Mulligan replied, looking more haggard and distraught than he ever had in the five years they'd been working together.

Alex was the lead researcher he'd hired only one month ago. The fifty-year-old robotics genius had been a critical part of the progress they'd recently made. "He's alive?"

Mike nodded. "Unconscious."

"Have the medics said anything?"

"He's breathing, and he's lost a lot of blood, but they were able to stabilize him," Mike said, his voice thin, watching as the medics rolled Alex out the door. "They're taking him to Harborview now."

Connor was relieved to hear that. "And the prototypes?"

"They're fine." Mike drew a breath and held it a moment before continuing. "The original is in the research lab, exactly where we left it, and the alarm is still set. The second one is safely locked in the basement."

"Then what happened here?"

"The alarm to your office tripped."

Concern flashed through Connor. "The safe?"

"Untouched."

Connor breathed a thankful sigh. "Have you checked the security video?"

"Disabled." Mike nodded toward Connor's office. "I need you to check your office to make sure nothing else is gone."

After a quick search, Connor agreed everything was where he'd left it. Turning to Mike, he threw up his hands. "I don't understand. Why go to all the trouble of a break-in and possibly risk assault or murder charges when they didn't take a thing?"

"I have two theories," Mike said as he leaned against the doorjamb.

"Let's hear them."

"All our security precautions stopped whoever broke in from getting the original white prototype or your research. Maybe they were after those things all along, and Alex just happened to be in the wrong place at the wrong time."

Nodding, Connor asked, "And your second theory?"

Mike frowned. "I suspect the burglar knew he'd never get close to either of those things and needed a distraction to grab something else that might induce you to hand it all over."

Connor went still. Ellie or his grandmother.

The two women were his greatest weaknesses. Connor grabbed his cell phone and dialed Ellie.

No answer.

Next he tried Grayson House.

No answer.

His heart pulsing in his ears, he tried his grandmother. He breathed a sigh of relief when she picked up on the second ring and assured him she was fine. He promised to call later and share more of the details when he knew what they were. Hanging up, he turned back to Mike. "Can you handle things here?"

"Of course. Are you headed home?"

He nodded. "I need to find Ellie. Call me with any updates on Alex."

"Will do. Good luck."

Connor placed one more call on his way back to the parking garage. "Trevor?"

"What's up? Are you calling to make sure I'm not going to back out of your invite to Thanksgiving dinner? I promised I'd be there."

"I need your help."

"With what?" Trevor asked.

"I'm not entirely sure yet, but I have a bad feeling something terrible has happened. Can you meet me at Grayson House?"

"Is this official police business?" Trevor asked.

"It might be."

"Be there in ten minutes."

Connor jumped into his fuel-efficient car. He drove faster than he normally would, leaving curses in his wake when lights slowed him down, until finally he pulled up in front of the house.

Trevor was already there, waiting outside. "What's up?"

"Nothing, I hope," he said as he strode up the front stairs. The door was ajar.

A sliver of apprehension moved through Connor.

"Behind me," Trevor said, pulling his gun. With his foot he moved the door open and entered the house, with Connor in his wake.

Instantly voices came at them from the hallway, the parlor, and the stairs. At the sight of Viola, Lenny, George, Ernie, and Aaron, as well as his father and Julie and James Hawthorne, Trevor holstered his gun. The din of their voices assailed Connor and Trevor all at once, the sound increasing until Connor released a shrill whistle, as though calling the troops to order.

A sudden silence fell over the grim-faced crowd.

"Why is everyone here?" Connor asked in frustration.

Viola leveled him with a frosty glare. "I called everyone after you called me and asked them all to meet here. If Ellie's in trouble, then it's up to her family to help get her out of it. Is Ellie in trouble? We searched the house and couldn't find her."

Connor looked at the people crowding the doorway, and despite his desperation to find Ellie, a sense of rightness came over him. Both he and Ellie had felt so alone all their lives, yet now that they'd found each other, they'd also found themselves surrounded by people who cared about them. "Yes, I believe Ellie is in trouble."

A collective gasp filled the room.

"We're going to find her. We'll bring her home, where she belongs," Connor said with determination.

"Are there any signs of a break-in? A struggle? Did you notice anything odd?" Trevor asked.

They all started talking at once.

Trevor moved up two stairs and turned. He raised his hands and said, "Quiet!"

They all stared at him, wide-eyed. Even without his uniform, Trevor had a commanding presence.

"Viola, tell me what you know so far," Trevor demanded.

"We arrived only moments before you. The front door was unlocked and partially open. We made an initial search of the house. The only thing I saw out of place was upstairs in the ballroom." Viola's face softened, and her gaze strayed to Lenny and Aaron, where they stood together. "Ellie did such a beautiful job with the decorations. It would be heartbreaking to let them go to waste." Her voice wavered.

"Don't worry, Grandmother. There will be a wedding on Friday with Ellie in attendance even if it takes me that long to find her," Connor vowed, then turned to Trevor. "I want to see what's upstairs."

Connor and Trevor climbed the grand staircase, taking two stairs at a time while the others followed more slowly. They entered the ballroom. Instead of seeing the beauty Ellie had created, Connor focused on the one out-of-place chair. "She was here, and she was taken."

Trevor frowned. "How can you be certain? All I see is a tipped-over chair."

"I've come to know her in the past five weeks, and she never would have left one chair askew. Look at the others. They're all perfectly aligned—to the millimeter. But not this one." Connor bent down and studied the chair more closely. "This would have driven Ellie crazy."

In his mind, Connor re-created the scene. "She was waiting for me to come home after a break-in was reported at the lab. We needed to talk." He stood, studying the chair from the top. "She sat in this chair, waiting."

Connor slowly walked to the door. "Something happened, maybe startling her. She got up, tipping the chair over as she moved to the door."

Trevor narrowed his gaze, mulling over Connor's theory. "You really think that's what—"

"Over here," Connor interrupted as he moved to the last row of chairs and bent down. Lying on the polished wooden floor was an abandoned syringe and hypodermic needle. He glanced back at Trevor as he tempered both panic and anger.

Trevor pulled an evidence bag from the pocket of his coat and scooped up the syringe, careful not to disturb any evidence that might be left behind. He sniffed the contents of the bag. "Smells like propofol. The anesthesia would have knocked her out instantly." To the others he said, "I've called for backup, but until the detectives arrive, I could use your help if you're willing to follow my directions."

"We'll do anything to help find our girl," James Hawthorne said, his voice deep with emotion.

Trevor took charge. "Search the room for other clues, but be careful not to touch anything. Call me if you see anything."

To James and Julie Hawthorne, Trevor said, "Would the two of you go downstairs and make a sweep for anything we missed?"

"What are we looking for?" James asked.

"Anything odd or out of place. But once again, I caution you not to disturb any possible evidence," Trevor implored.

With a nod, they hurried from the room.

Viola and the Elvises started at the front of the ballroom. Only the slowness of Viola's movements betrayed the fact she was still recovering.

When the others were out of earshot, Connor pulled his cell phone from his pocket and stared at the blank screen. Clenching his teeth, he said, "Why doesn't whoever took her contact me?"

"They will when they're ready."

Connor released a growl. "I never was very good at waiting."

"She's safe for now."

"How can you be sure?"

"They need her alive to bargain with you. Make sure you ask to talk to her when they do call."

"And after we make whatever deal they want?"

Trevor's face fell. "That's when we have to worry."

Viola and the men had finished their inspection and returned with no further clues. When he saw Viola leaning heavily on Aaron's arm for support, Connor pulled one of the chairs from its row and offered it to his grandmother.

With a grateful smile, she sat. "Have you been contacted by anyone yet?"

Connor shook his head and returned his phone to his pocket.

"I'll pay whatever they want," Viola said with feeling as she regained some strength.

"We'll help," the Elvises replied at once, taking up positions around Viola, as though guarding her from whatever danger had swallowed Ellie.

James and Julie returned to the ballroom. "We can help, too," Ellie's father said, his face ashen. "We bought trip insurance for our cruise. All we have to do is cancel, and we can come up with several thousand to help our little girl."

Connor looked down at James's hand. He held a small envelope between a tissue and his index finger and thumb. "Did you find something?"

James extended the envelope toward Connor. "We found this near the door, like it had been slipped beneath."

"Wait," Trevor said as Connor went to grab it. He removed a pair of latex gloves from his pocket and put them on before he took the envelope from James. Carefully, Trevor broke the seal and peered inside.

"What is it?" Connor asked, his throat tight. It had to be about Ellie. *It has to be.*

Slowly Trevor removed several strands of burnished-gold hair and held them up. "Is it Ellie's?"

"Yes," Connor ground out.

"Oh, dear God," Viola cried as she collapsed back against her chair.

"My baby," Julie sobbed, dabbing at her eyes with a handkerchief. "I just want her back."

"We'll find her," Trevor assured them as he pulled out his cell phone. "I'll have someone at the station run a trace on her phone. She hasn't been missing for twenty-four hours yet, but the evidence found here suggests this is a crime, not a missing person's case. I'm setting up a police team now."

Connor felt as if his heart were being squeezed in a vise. He forced himself to think past the pain, ignoring the panic that threatened to drown him. "Why don't you all go home? We'll let you know when we hear something."

Connor shifted his gaze from the fear and desperation in Ellie's parents' eyes to his father's determined expression. "We'll find her, son."

Connor looked to his left, to the Elvises.

Lenny frowned and shook his head. Speaking for his friends, he said, "The Elvises are staying put."

He turned to Viola. Her face became mutinous. "Don't think for one minute since I'm old and feeble that I can't stay up and wait with you. I care about that girl as much as any of you."

The assembled group murmured sounds of affirmation, and Connor knew he'd lost that battle before it had even started. "All right. We'll wait this out together. But there are six bedrooms in this house if anyone needs to rest."

No one replied, and not one of the faces that stared back at him looked as if they'd be giving in to sleep anytime soon.

For better or for worse, they were all in this together.

CHAPTER
TWENTY-ONE

The text came at midnight, demanding his prototype and his research in exchange for Ellie.

They wanted everything he had to give on the self-driving car. Connor would hand it over willingly if it kept Ellie safe and brought her back to the people who loved her.

No one had gone to bed. Those assembled sat at attention now as the hostage-negotiation team Trevor had brought in coached Connor on what to say in order to secure a transfer location place and time, as well as demand visual proof Ellie was unharmed.

Show me proof she's all right. Connor typed onto the screen.

Do what we ask and she will be.

Connor could feel the frustration searing inside him, stronger than ever. Show me Ellie.

You don't need proof besides her hair.

Like hell I don't. Connor typed the reply and hit "Send," praying he'd made his point.

One hour. The reply came; then his cell phone went silent.

◆ ◆ ◆

After what seemed like hours, Ellie finally managed to loosen the knot at her hands and slip her wrists free. She took a moment to massage her abused flesh, then worked on untying her feet. As soon as she was free, she stood.

She wobbled on her feet—proof that the effects of the drugs Amanda had given her weren't entirely out of her system yet. But she couldn't wait until they were. If she was going to make a break for her freedom, it had to be now.

Her heart thundering in her ears, she groped through the darkness to her left. Ellie followed the image she'd burned in her mind of the location of the door. When she came to a wall, she put out her hands and fumbled her way along the cool concrete, desperate to find the door. Finally she came to what felt like the frame of a single metal door.

It took her a moment to locate the door handle. She pushed, then pushed harder, only to confirm it was locked.

She drew a fortifying breath. Determined to set herself free, she moved along the wall in the opposite direction. While the lantern had been lit, she hadn't had a clear view of what was on the right side of the chamber. With luck, perhaps she'd come upon a door that was unlocked or a window she could break.

She hadn't made it far when the grinding noise of the lock sliding free filled the silence. The door beside her slowly opened.

A chill went up her spine.

Amanda had returned.

Ellie froze. She had to act now.

Pale-yellow light spilled into the darkness, giving her a view of the door as it opened. Ellie kicked the metal with her right foot, forcing the door to slam into Amanda. She dropped the lantern and shrieked as the metal door connected with her perfect face.

Adrenaline pumped through Ellie. She stepped around the front of the door and swung at the startled Amanda, catching her in the head. Instead of lunging backward like she expected, Amanda dove for Ellie, grabbing her by the hair.

Ellie ducked, twisted. Her hair slipped from Amanda's grasp. Instantly, Amanda lashed something around Ellie's neck and held tight.

Panic flooded Ellie as she clawed at Amanda's fingers. She needed air every bit as much as she needed a way to escape. If only she could break free, she might be able to clear the doorway. Then she could run, and keep on running.

Ellie could feel herself weakening as her lungs burned. In a desperate attempt for breath, Ellie knocked her head back into Amanda's.

"Stop fighting me," Amanda growled as she loosened her grip, giving Ellie a chance to suck in much-needed air. But before she could run, Amanda shoved the barrel of a gun against Ellie's rib cage. "I'll shoot."

Ellie froze. She might long to be free, but she also had no wish to die.

"How did you untie yourself?"

She pressed her lips tight.

"Oh, never mind. There's no way out of here except through me, so start cooperating." The half-light from the lantern was enough to illuminate the anger in Amanda's eyes.

With her semiautomatic pistol, she motioned for Ellie to step back against the wall. Her nose was bleeding, and Ellie had managed to cut Amanda's left cheek. Neither slowed her down.

"Here's what we're going to do," Amanda said. "We're going to make a phone call. The only words you will say are 'I'm fine. Give them what they want.' That's it. Nothing more or I'll shoot you, and Loverboy will see every gory detail. Understand?"

Amanda was calling Connor? Ellie racked her brain, trying to figure out how to convey more in the message without tipping Amanda off.

Amanda stepped back and righted the lantern, casting more light around the room and on Ellie. She pulled a cell phone from her jacket. With the phone in one hand and the gun in the other, she turned the camera on Ellie.

Ellie knew after their tussle she must look disheveled. She didn't want Connor to worry, so she lifted her chin and tried to look confident. "I'm fine." She hesitated as her brain scrambled for a way to warn him who held her captive. "Give her what she wants."

Amanda ended the call and threw the cell phone against the wall, shattering it into a hundred pieces.

Ellie tensed as the phone splintered across the floor, fearing Amanda had noticed the subtle change she'd made to the message.

Then Amanda smiled. "Very good. Now we wait."

Ellie released a pent-up breath. Amanda hadn't noticed. Then in an attempt at bravado, Ellie hitched her chin up another notch. "What if Connor doesn't meet your demands?"

Amanda moved back to where she'd originally dumped Ellie and snatched up a length of rope. "If he doesn't, then it's bye-bye Ellie."

Amanda motioned for her to turn around, then jammed her against the wall while she tied her hands behind her back. "There, that should keep you out of trouble."

She picked up the lantern and drew out another cell phone from her coat pocket. She typed in something, then put the phone back in her pocket before heading for the door.

"Please . . . leave the light," Ellie asked, the words fracturing as a ripple of fear chased across her nerves.

"No."

The word echoed in the stillness of the room as Amanda closed and locked the door, pitching Ellie into darkness once more.

◆ ◆ ◆

Give her what she wants?

"Anything? Any ideas who has Ellie?" Trevor asked as the connection went dead.

"I know who has Ellie. Amanda Frost."

"Your old girlfriend?" Trevor asked. "The one who stole your research and prototype once before?"

Connor nodded.

"Run her name. Let's see what she's been up to lately," Trevor said to his team before his gaze returned to Connor. "Anything else you can tell me that would be helpful?"

"There's not much to tell. I hadn't seen Amanda since college. Then four weeks ago, she appeared at a party Ellie and I attended."

"Okay. Let's see what comes up in the computer. Meanwhile, we'll run her plates and get her cell-phone records," Trevor said with a worried frown.

"I never should have left Ellie alone," Connor said, raking his hands through his hair, trying desperately to hold back his frustration, his fear.

"Don't do that to yourself, man. You had no way of knowing."

The pain of his mistake was enough to cripple him. "I should have been more suspicious of why Amanda suddenly reappeared in Seattle. Her company is based in San Francisco. Some people don't change." He hadn't changed either until . . . Ellie. Five weeks ago he hadn't believed in love. He hadn't believed in happy endings. He'd never wanted to share his life with anyone or grow old together.

Until her.

Life without Ellie wasn't something he wanted to contemplate. He would give everything he had to get her back. His self-driving car was, after all, simply a car. Ellie was priceless.

His heart screamed the truth. He loved her more than he'd ever loved anyone or anything else in his life.

"Let's get everything we need to make the exchange," Connor said to Trevor. "They sent us the drop location. I'm going to give them everything."

CHAPTER
TWENTY-TWO

Four hours later, Connor parked the white prototype in front of the Museum of Flight, as directed, in the space between the two orange construction cones. Since it was five in the morning on Thanksgiving Day and the museum was closed, no one was around in the big, open parking lot.

Connor stepped from the car. A chill abraded his exposed skin. He flipped up the collar of his shearling-lined coat against the November wind as he searched the surrounding airpark with careful eyes in the early-morning light. Ellie would be here somewhere.

Frustration coiled inside him. There were so many planes.

The final instructions were to park the car between the orange cones and to retrieve Ellie from one of the planes in the airpark. Was she not near a plane but inside it? He'd search them all if he had to.

"Walk away from the prototype," Trevor said in his earpiece. "Follow the plan. You get the girl. I'll follow the car."

Connor's feet moved along the sidewalk to the north side of the entrance, but his brain had kicked into overdrive, scanning the planes. His head pounded in time with his pulse. Where was she?

He turned to the new covered section of the airpark as he inspected the SST. Not there. Then his heart soared at the sight of her burnished hair in the cockpit of a B-17. "She's in the green B-17 off to my right."

"Is she"—Trevor hesitated—"alive?"

"She's slumped forward, not moving." His heart in his throat, he broke into a run. She'd placed Ellie farther away from the prototype, most likely so she could get to the car before he could reach Ellie.

"Get ready, team," Trevor said.

Out of the corner of his eye, Connor saw Amanda separate herself from one of the nearby jumbo jets on display. She raced to the car and hopped in. Wouldn't she be surprised when she discovered how slowly the car moved? He hadn't adjusted the navigation system back from accuracy to speed. Connor would have allowed himself a wicked grin if he wasn't so concerned for Ellie's safety. He really didn't care if Trevor recovered the prototype or if he arrested Amanda. All his thoughts were of Ellie.

Adrenaline hit his system like a freight train, pushing him forward. He couldn't reach the cockpit from the front, so he ran around to the wing. He jumped up and ran along the fuselage to the cockpit windows. Ellie was hunched over the control panel. Her hair fell across her face, and for a moment he wondered if they'd been tricked—if this wasn't really Ellie at all.

Forcing his panic aside, he peered through the glass at the woman inside. Her hair was pushed to one side, exposing her ear. His heart cried out at the sight of a familiar freckle on the base of the lobe. It was Ellie inside, but was she alive, breathing?

Desperate to reach her, he raced down the wing and jumped down, heading to the waist gunner door. He pulled the hatch lock. It was either stuck or blocked. Unwilling to be defeated, Connor spread his legs wide, giving himself the most leverage possible, and wrenched the hatch lock to the open position. A pop sounded; then whatever was blocking it fell free. He swung the hatch up and went inside.

Quickly he worked his way through the airplane, heading toward the cockpit. When he reached Ellie, he knelt beside her and placed two fingers across the carotid artery of her neck. His breath stopped when he didn't pick up a pulse. Moving his fingers closer to her windpipe, he released his breath in a rush as a weak pulse beat against his fingers. Mentally giving thanks, he cradled her cheek in his hand. "I've got you, love."

They'd most likely drugged her with the same sedative as before. But it didn't matter. He'd found her. She was alive. They could deal with the rest. Hope sprang to life within him. A bright flame that warmed him from within.

He clung to that sensation as he scooped Ellie into his arms and headed for the gunner door. Help was nearby. "Trevor. Send in the medic unit. Ellie's alive but not responsive."

"On its way," Trevor replied. "Hang in there."

He strode through the plane, and by the time he made it outside, the medic team was there with a stretcher. Connor placed Ellie on it, then reluctantly released her as the medics hooked her up to oxygen and started an IV. Once they were satisfied she was stable, they wheeled her inside the ambulance.

Connor got in and sat beside her, holding her hand once more as they made their way to Swedish Hospital. As the medics worked, Connor bent close to Ellie's ear. "I want to change the terms of our agreement. Come back to me, Ellie."

◆ ◆ ◆

Connor paced outside Ellie's hospital room anxiously. The medics assured him she would be fine. If that were so, then why didn't she wake up?

"Connor?"

He turned at the sound of Jordan's voice. Before he realized what he was doing, he pulled the physician's assistant into a hug, then released her. "Thank goodness you're here. Can you please tell me why Ellie won't wake up?"

Jordan met his gaze with a curious light in her eyes. "You really do care about her, don't you?"

"Of course I do. She's my wife."

Jordan smiled. "I can see why Ellie likes you."

At his puzzled expression, Jordan laughed.

"She's going to be fine," Jordan said. "The drugs should work their way out of her system fairly soon. I suggest you stay close."

"I'm not leaving her side." He looked past Jordan as Trevor came to join them.

"It's all done," Trevor said. "Amanda Frost is in the King County jail awaiting arraignment, and your prototype is back at your lab, courtesy of Mike Mulligan."

Connor clapped Trevor on the back. "Thanks, man. Not sure what I would've done without your help."

"I'll have to think of a way for you to pay me back." Trevor smiled mischievously as he turned toward Jordan. "We haven't met." He held out his hand. "Trevor Edwards, SPD."

Her green eyes raked him from head to toe. "Jordan Krane, PA dash C."

Connor sighed and shook his head. "You two play alphabet soup for now, but I expect to see both of you at Grayson House tomorrow. Thanksgiving Day is a bust, but the wedding is on. Ellie and I would love our best friends to be there."

Trevor's dark eyes filled with interest. "Wouldn't miss it for the world."

◆ ◆ ◆

Ellie opened her eyes and stared up at the bag of saline solution hanging over her head. She frowned. When had she gotten an IV?

She heard voices. One of them distinct from the others.

"Connor?"

Soft footsteps sounded, and he was beside her. "Welcome back," he said in a soothing voice.

An inexplicable feeling of joy moved through her at the sight of his face above her. He reached down and cupped her face with his hands and kissed her deeply.

Then just as quickly, the joy vanished, replaced with fear. "Amanda?" she asked as she looked beyond Connor to see she was in a hospital room. "What happened?"

"Amanda was caught before she even left the parking lot. You remember how slow the car moves? She had no idea her plan was doomed to failure by using the prototype as her getaway car."

Ellie released a soft laugh. "That kind of makes me feel a little sorry for her."

"Don't feel sorry for Amanda. She got what she deserved." Connor gently stroked Ellie's cheek with his thumb. "Now, back to us. We never finished our discussion."

Before Ellie could comment, a commotion came from the doorway. "She's awake? Let us through." Her bearing as regal as ever, Viola crossed to the bed and took up a position across from Connor, folding her in an exuberant hug. "My darling girl, I was so worried about you. I'm grateful beyond words that you're safe."

James and Julie Hawthorne crowded around the opposite side of the bed. "The best outcome possible. Thanks for bringing her back to us, Connor." Ellie's father shook Connor's hand, treating him as if he were a conquering hero.

"What did I miss after Amanda drugged me a second time?" Ellie asked, her gaze shifting back to Connor.

He gave her a smile. "I'll explain everything to you . . . later."

The Elvises entered the room, wreathed in smiles. "We could tell when we first met you that you were a fighter," Lenny said as he bent to kiss her bruised cheek.

Aaron, Ernie, and George crowded in. "We're so glad you're okay," Aaron said with a heartfelt smile.

"I'm so happy to see you all, and I thank you for your concern and your love. And since you're all here, there is one thing we need to talk about." Again, her gaze found Connor's.

"My dear," Viola interrupted, "the only thing we need to discuss is how quickly you'll be out of this hospital bed. We all missed Thanksgiving because we were so concerned for your safety, but now that you're better, I'd love to get married, and then there's the Holiday Street of Dreams that starts tomorrow. None of those things can happen without you."

"I need to know something first, before any of this goes any further." Ellie pulled herself up into a sitting position. Her hands tightened on the handrails as she fought another bout of dizziness. She had to say what had been haunting her since before Amanda had kidnapped her. "What role did you all play in Connor's and my relationship?"

Viola and the Elvises fixed her with identical inquiring looks. "What are you talking about, dear?" Viola asked.

Ellie knew she should rest, but she had to know the truth. "I've never been drugged before last night, or so I thought." She glanced at Lenny, George, Ernie, and Aaron. "What did you all do the night Connor and I got married?"

Ashen faces stared back.

"You're asking if we drugged you? The answer is no," Lenny said, his features as serious as she'd ever seen them. "Did we do what we could to fan the flames of love? Yes. We knew about your past together, and we knew you were both in town. All we had to do was make sure you both stayed in the same hotel, and that you happened to meet in the hotel bar."

Ellie's gaze clashed with Connor's. "Did you receive an offer in the mail for a free hotel room that just happened to be one of the dates you'd be in town?"

"Yes," he said. "I took advantage of that offer. Did you also get a voucher for a free drink in the lobby bar with the same deal?" he asked Ellie.

Ellie wanted to be mad about how easily she'd allowed herself to be manipulated, but it was hard when the chain of events had led her to this moment—and to the one man she'd never been able to forget. "You four should be ashamed of yourselves."

Lenny's shoulders slumped. "We might have overstepped our bounds there a bit, but it was only because we wanted you both to know how perfect you are for each other."

Ellie narrowed her gaze on the contrite men. "What else did you do?"

A flush crept over George's cheeks. "The flowers, the love notes you thought were from Connor . . . and the sheet music you thought was from Ellie . . ."

Connor's lips thinned. "You didn't think I could romance my wife myself?"

Ernie wrung his hands before him. "We should have trusted you two to find your own way."

"How did you get them in the house?" Ellie asked.

"Viola gave us a key to the kitchen door." Lenny reached inside his T-shirt for a key on a silver chain. "We're sorry," he said, his face filled with remorse as he slipped the chain over his head and handed the key to Connor. Lenny hesitated as he looked at the other three Elvises. "We didn't drug you or manipulate you in any way to get you to the altar. You two were eager enough to get there all on your own."

Connor looked from the Elvises to his grandmother. The betrayal in his eyes was tangible for a heartbeat; then as quickly as it had appeared, it was gone. He turned back to Ellie and took her hand. "Are you mad about us meeting and getting married?"

"I should be mad. I don't like being deceived or manipulated," Ellie said, looking straight at Viola. The older woman winced but remained silent.

"But you're not, right?" Connor asked with hope in his voice.

Ellie stared at the people gathered around her bed. Their faces were a mixture of confusion and remorse and love. Did she care how she and Connor had come together? Or who manipulated whom?

She looked up into Connor's green eyes. He looked at her with love, a deep and abiding love that no one could have fabricated.

The thought invigorated her. Did she care? Heck no. When she'd been alone in the darkness of the warehouse, all she'd thought about were the moments she and Connor had shared.

"What about our agreement?" she asked.

"The only agreement I'll settle on is that you're part of my life forever, Mrs. Grayson."

"You're certain? Because as you know, no Hawthorne has ever been divorced."

He gave her his most devastating smile and bent to kiss her. "I have never been more certain of anything in my life."

"I think that's our cue to leave," Viola said, ushering the others out of the hospital room. At the door she turned back. "Wedding tomorrow at ten?"

"Grayson House opens at ten to the public," Ellie replied, still trying to recover from the impact of Connor's kiss.

Viola arched her brow. "It's only fitting that we start the holiday showing of the house with a celebration this city won't soon forget."

"When are you going to tell us who your bridegroom is?" Connor asked.

"I can't tell you now." A smug smile pulled up her lips. "You need incentive to get out of that bed. I'll see you tomorrow morning at Grayson House."

When she was gone, Connor turned to Ellie and lifted her chin with the arc of his fingers. His lips descended, his mouth moving over hers, claiming her, and telling her all the things he had not yet said—that he loved her, needed her, wanted her. For the two of them, after all they'd been through, love could be communicated in no other way. It was an emotion that didn't need sound; it needed action.

Connor had shown her his love by sacrificing everything for her. He'd willingly handed over the things she thought he'd held most dear.

She'd been wrong.

His kiss told her that love, their love, was powerful, all-consuming, and triumphant. They had both needed to surrender themselves and all they held precious to realize what they meant to each other.

After a long while, Connor pulled back, but kept his hand at her cheek.

"Want to stay here tonight?" he asked, his words heavy with desire. "Or would you like me to see what I can do about getting you discharged?"

"I want to go home. With you."

His hand fell away from her face. They shared a smile without speaking what was in both of their hearts. "Let me go find Jordan. She'll be pleased to know you're awake and ready to be set free."

Ellie watched Connor walk out of the room, leaving her alone with her thoughts. They would have to talk soon about what their future would hold.

A future with Connor.

Five weeks ago, Connor and her staying together seemed impossible. After what they'd lived through in the last several hours, losing him was not something she wished to contemplate. It was certainly not something she would accept.

CHAPTER
TWENTY-THREE

"We did it," Ellie said in awe as she stood beside Connor outside Grayson House, their breath curling in the chill morning air.

Sunshine glimmered off a light dusting of snow that had fallen in the last hour, covering the roof and the lawn, turning an already beautiful house into a fairytale setting.

"It's not just a house—it's magical," Ellie said with a smile. The nineteenth-century mansion looked better than any other house on the street.

"It's Christmas and family and love all rolled up in a pretty pink package," Connor said.

He put into words the emotions inside her. Grayson House was a home—their home for one more day.

"Let's get you out of the cold," Connor said. With a hand at the small of her back, he ushered her up the stairs to the door.

Zanzibar waited for them in the foyer. At their entrance, the cat padded over to Connor and rubbed against his legs. A soft purring sound filled the air.

"Someone is happy you're home," Ellie giggled.

"That makes two of us. I'm happy you're home and safe," he said, yet worry reflected in his eyes.

Knowing there was more to be said, Ellie said, "But . . ."

Connor released a heavy sigh and waved her into the parlor. "I know you must be exhausted, but we're finally going to have that talk. No matter what." He took a seat on the settee.

She settled onto the settee across from him. To her surprise, Zanzibar jumped into her lap, curled up, and went to sleep. Exhaustion should have overcome her by now, but she was far too awake to contemplate sleep. Ellie summoned a grateful smile. "Thank you for everything you did to negotiate my release."

Connor frowned. "You were only in trouble because of me and my connection to Amanda."

Ellie shrugged. "What relationship isn't a little bit complicated?"

He raised a brow. "I'd say being kidnapped and drugged goes well beyond complicated and into dangerous."

She fixed Connor with an uncompromising gaze. "You're worth any danger that might come our way."

"If you want to get married again, without the Elvises, we can," he said, his smile fading. "I want you to have the wedding you've always wanted."

"It's the person you marry who matters, not the wedding itself." She set Zanzibar on the floor, then stood as she closed the space between herself and Connor. "There is one last thing I want you to know, to really understand if we are to be husband and wife."

She paused while he stood and looked into her eyes.

"I'll never leave you," she said.

"I believe you not only because it's you who's saying it but also because I've put my past to rest." At her incredulous look, he continued. "I found out why my mother left my father and me."

"How? Why?" she asked in a disbelieving breath.

"Trevor helped," Connor explained. "He found a hospice nurse who remembered my mother."

"Hospice?"

Connor nodded, then explained all he'd learned about Mary Grayson.

Tears pooled in Ellie's eyes, falling onto her cheeks. "Does it help to talk about her?"

"With you, yes." Connor reached up and brushed her tears away. "I want to talk about anything and everything with you for years to come."

She swallowed roughly. "What are you saying?"

His green eyes filled with an emotion she hadn't seen in them before. "I love you, Ellie." He reached for the divorce papers on the table beside them and ripped them in half.

Tossing them aside, he caught her to him, bent his head, and kissed her. This kiss was not to woo her. This kiss was meant to show her how much she meant to him. How much he wanted her, needed her, desired her. To show her heaven was within their reach.

After a while he pulled back, keeping her in his arms. "Can we talk about one more thing?"

"What's left to discuss?"

"The honeymoon your parents are determined to give us?"

Ellie laughed. "Let's go anywhere but Vegas."

"How does Bora-Bora sound?" Connor asked with a lift of his brow.

"Romantic."

He brought his lips to hers, and their exchange went on until that all-consuming passion flared to life between them.

Even as passion fired her blood, Ellie knew something between them was different. She couldn't name exactly what it was, for it was only a feeling. A sense really, of something special—the thread of a promise that wove them together for all eternity.

Closing her eyes, Ellie drew in that power with every racing beat of her heart as he pulled her close, crushing her breasts, already peaked and tight and aching, to the hard, solid planes of his chest. With his hands, he possessed her, sculpting her curves.

They had married in Las Vegas. They might have even had a wedding night there. But this moment was the two of them coming together as one.

Slowly he broke their kiss and pulled back.

She opened her eyes and looked up at him.

"I want you so badly it hurts, but not here. I want you in our bed, today and for the rest of our days." His thumb moved over her fingers as though unwilling to break their connection entirely.

Ellie nodded. She would gladly follow him upstairs or anywhere he asked at the moment.

Taking her hand, he led her up the stairs to the master bedroom. Stopping beside the bed, he brought both of his hands up to frame her face, tipped it up to his, and looked into her eyes. "I would have given everything I owned for you."

"I know that now." She rose up on her toes, bringing their lips together once more.

Their hunger for each other reignited as if there'd been no pause. Greedily she let him taste her, allowing a familiar tide to sweep them away.

Needing the feel of his skin beneath her fingertips, Ellie untucked his shirt and ran her hands underneath, branding his skin with her own as she pushed the fabric of his shirt over his head, then tossed the garment aside.

He bent to kiss her neck, then her shoulder, as he slowly lifted her sweater along her torso and over her head. Her bra followed, and her breasts sprang free. He reached for her, his eyes dark with passion, as he traced her every curve, possessing every inch of her body.

Their breathing ragged and desperate for more, they dispensed of their clothing until they stood naked with no barriers to their love.

Needing the promise of his body against hers, Ellie arched against him, and reaching down, she filled her hand with his heavy erection. Curling her palm around his warmth, she stroked up, then down with her thumb. "I love how you feel in my hands."

He shuddered and wrapped his arms around her waist. Now in charge of their lovemaking, he lowered her to the bed and leaned over her. He ran his hands over her body, teasing until he'd reduced her to a state of panting need.

Then he moved over her, parted her legs with his hard, muscled thighs, and with one powerful thrust, he filled her.

She arched beneath him as he completed her. They gave themselves over to desire as they were intimately joined, two hearts beating together, racing toward ecstasy.

Their passion leaped higher as they clung together, at the mercy of the other, eager to gain what they'd evoked, until finally, raw sensation flared, sharpened, and shattered.

Connor cried out, his voice merging with her own as a glorious rapture consumed them.

As they floated back to earth in each other's arms, Ellie knew beyond a doubt that she belonged with this man, that their future was together, and that she could trust him not only with her body but also with her heart.

◆ ◆ ◆

Early-morning light shone through the window when Connor finally stirred the next day. He smiled down at the woman who lay curled in his arms. He felt her closeness down to the marrow of his bones.

They'd made love several times during what had remained of the day and into the night. Now that they were committed to each other, their passion seemed to have no end.

He was tempted to wake her now and explore some part of her body he had yet to discover, except that they were expecting visitors very soon. Not only would the wedding party descend upon them, but the house would open for the Holiday Street of Dreams in less than two hours.

Slowly extricating his arm from beneath her head, he slipped from the bed. She could sleep a bit longer while he took care of a few last-minute details.

When he returned to the master bedroom forty minutes later, Ellie was still asleep. He bent down and pressed a kiss to her cheek, then pushed aside her hair, revealing the small freckle on her earlobe. He kissed that, too. "Good morning, my wife."

Her eyes snapped open. "Morning!" She bolted upright in bed, nearly spilling the breakfast tray he'd brought her. She reached out, righting the orange juice before it tipped. "What time is it?"

He smiled at the vision before him. Her hair was a wild mass of tangles, and her cheeks were flushed from the aftermath of their love-making. "You have time for breakfast and a shower."

Her eyes flared wide. "But the hologram needs—"

"I set it up."

"The ballroom?"

He smiled. "Finished."

Her brows came together as she sniffed the air. "The cookies?"

"Done."

A look of amazement came over her face. "The caterers?"

"They're in the kitchen." He sat on the bed beside her. "All you need to do is eat and get dressed at your leisure for the wedding."

A radiant smile spread across her face. "What did I do to deserve you?"

"You're just lucky, I guess," he said before he bent and snatched another kiss from her lips.

◆ ◆ ◆

She was lucky, all right, Ellie thought to herself an hour later as she made her way downstairs. In the foyer she stopped and marveled once again at the changes she and Connor had brought to Grayson House. The scents of pine and freshly baked cookies filled her senses, and they made the house feel homey and festive at the same time.

Turning around the foyer, she took in the Christmas tree with its twinkling lights; the garlands sweeping up the staircase, giving the house an extra touch of elegance; the bright-red walls; and the grandfather clock against them.

She looked at the old man's face. She blinked, not believing her eyes. When she looked at him again, nothing had changed.

Yet she'd swear, for a moment, the old man had been smiling.

CHAPTER
TWENTY-FOUR

At 9:55 a.m., Ellie hurried into the already crowded ballroom. She'd dressed in her favorite dove-gray sheath dress because it accentuated the silver-and-aquamarine necklace Viola had given her perfectly.

"Is everything all right?" Connor asked, his voice filled with concern. His eyes moved to her legs, and desire flared in the dark-green depths.

Ellie slipped into the seat beside him in the front row and sat back against the chair, grateful for the momentary respite. "I'm a little frazzled from running up and down the stairs, trying to make sure both the open house and the wedding are on schedule." Connor had dressed in a tuxedo for the day. He looked every bit as handsome as she remembered from their wedding photos.

He took her hand and gave it a squeeze. "You've done an excellent job with both, Ellie."

Looking behind her, Ellie saw that Olivia and Max sat together, and Connor's friend Trevor sat beside Jordan. The two had their heads close, talking as if they'd been friends forever. Ellie turned back to Connor. "Did you set Trevor and Jordan up?"

Connor shrugged. "I introduced them yesterday."

Ellie leaned into Connor and pressed a kiss to his cheek. "You're the best."

"I didn't do anything. You're the one who's created all the magic in this house."

The wedding had garnered the attention of the press and the public. The first row in the ballroom had been reserved for family. The next two were filled with journalists, TV crews, and photographers. All the other rows were filled with friends, neighbors, and curious Seattleites.

She smiled. "I admit, this is the fun part, after all the work is done, sitting back and watching it all happen."

"Nothing's going to happen without Viola." Connor frowned. "Where is she?"

"You know your grandmother." Ellie gave him a knowing look. "She's milking the attention for all she can."

He raised a brow.

"She's at the front door in her bridal gown, greeting every visitor to the house as a guest to the wedding."

"It's almost ten," Connor said, looking at his watch.

"Don't worry. I doubt Viola has missed a cue in her whole life."

Less than two minutes later, Ellie squeezed Connor's hand. "Here she comes."

A whisper rustled through the ballroom as first Lenny as Red Elvis, then George as White Elvis, and finally Ernie as Gold Elvis entered the room and took up their positions. George was the officiant, Lenny was the best man, and Ernie was the Elvis of honor, as he liked to call himself.

"She's marrying Aaron," Connor whispered in Ellie's ear. "Did you know?"

Ellie shook her head. No one but Viola knew what was in her heart. "I'm sure Aaron's very happy."

"Are we going to have to deal with three broken hearts when this is over?"

Ellie's gaze strayed to where all of Viola's friends from her retirement center were seated. All six of them had had their hair done and had dressed in their finest holiday attire. They looked at the wedding party with intense interest. "I'd say Lenny, George, and Ernie are going to have to watch out or they'll find themselves married before the end of the year."

Lenny, George, and Ernie started singing "Nothing's Going to Keep Me from You" as Viola walked down the aisle with a beaming Aaron on her arm. At the altar, Viola and Aaron joined in, entertaining the crowd as they must have in the past.

"That's not an Elvis song," Ellie said with a hint of amusement.

Connor laughed. "Lenny told me it was my grandmother's signature song when they performed in Vegas years ago."

"They're amazing," Ellie whispered.

"Viola always was full of surprises."

When they were through, the audience was on its feet, clapping.

"It wouldn't surprise me at all if they got job offers to start a new act right here in Seattle from this," Connor exclaimed.

"Who knew they had such talent?" Ellie's eyes were stinging with tears as she rose to her feet, applauding with the crowd.

"They aren't the only ones who will gain notoriety from this performance." Connor grinned.

"What do you mean?"

He pulled back to look in her eyes. "I have a feeling your business opportunities are going to be many in the coming weeks. You can't buy this kind of publicity. The reasons that sent you to Las Vegas five weeks ago are about to come true."

"At the time, I thought work was what I wanted. Instead, I got what I needed."

"What was that?" he asked, giving her a smile that made her strong and weak at the same time.

"Best gamble of my life. I got you, Mr. Grayson."

Connor tucked her hand into his lap and held tight as they watched the rest of the wedding in silence. When the wedding ended, the attendees shifted from the front of the ballroom to the back. A champagne brunch buffet waited there.

Instead of heading directly to the receiving line, Viola drifted toward her and Connor.

"How are you?" Viola asked Ellie with compassion in her voice.

"I couldn't be better." Ellie slipped her arm around her husband. "I know you and Aaron are leaving for your honeymoon later today. Connor and I will make sure we have our things moved out before you return."

"Whatever for?"

"So you and Aaron can move in."

With a smug look, Viola said, "Aaron's moving in with me at the retirement center."

"Then what will happen to Grayson House?" Connor asked. "You can't leave it empty again. The house deserves to be filled with people who love living there."

"I agree. My lawyer, Georgia Burke, will be in contact with you both tomorrow. I've had all the papers drawn up," Viola said, a gleam of mischief in her eyes. "I'm giving the house to the two of you."

Tears of happiness filled Ellie's eyes. The same emotions swelled in her chest, and filled her heart to overflowing. She pulled Viola close for a hug. "Nothing would make us happier."

When Viola pulled back, her gaze passed between Ellie and Connor. "I have only one request."

"We'll do anything for you, Grandmother. Won't we, Ellie?"

There was a time not long ago when she would have at least tensed at Viola's unknown request. Now she simply smiled. "Anything at all."

"Love each other," Viola said, her blue eyes peaceful and calm.

"Always," Ellie said.

"No problem there," Connor replied.

"Good." Viola looked out across the crowd until she found Aaron. "My husband is waiting. I have no idea how many days either of us has left on this earth, but I intend to enjoy every one of them." She fluttered her fingers at them as she walked toward Aaron.

Ellie stared after Viola for a moment, then turned to Connor. "She gave us this house." Ellie's voice was filled with awe.

A heartbeat passed as he framed her face with his hands. "She gave us her legacy." He studied her eyes and, lowering his head, brushed her lips with his. "Welcome to Grayson House, Mrs. Grayson."

Ellie pressed up on her toes and brought her lips to his, knowing to the core of her being that there really was such a thing as happily ever after.

A RECIPE FOR YOU
FROM ELLIE'S GRANDMOTHER

Gingerbread Cookies

1/2 cup butter, softened
3/4 cup packed dark-brown sugar
1/3 cup molasses
1 large egg
2 tablespoons water
2 2/3 cups all-purpose flour
2 teaspoons ground ginger
1 teaspoon baking soda
1/2 teaspoon salt
1/2 teaspoon each ground cinnamon, nutmeg, and allspice

In a large bowl, cream butter and brown sugar until light and fluffy. Beat in molasses, egg, and water. In a separate bowl, combine flour, ginger, baking soda, salt, cinnamon, nutmeg, and allspice; add to creamed mixture and mix well. Divide dough in half. Cover and refrigerate 30 minutes or until easy to handle.

Preheat oven to 350 degrees. On a lightly floured surface, roll out each portion of dough to 1/8-inch thickness. Cut with a floured 4-inch cookie cutter, or cut into side and roof pieces for a gingerbread house. Place 2 inches apart on greased baking sheets. Reroll scraps.

Bake 8–10 minutes or until edges are firm. Remove to wire racks to cool completely. Decorate as desired.

Yield: About 2 dozen cookies or 1 gingerbread house

ACKNOWLEDGMENTS

With the deepest appreciation to my fabulous Montlake team: Maria, Melody, Robin, Hai-Yen, Jessica, Mikyla, Ahn, and Marlene. I am eternally grateful to each of you. And to my agent, Pamela Ahearn, thank you for your guidance and your friendship.

Thank you, also, to a very special group of women: Sheila, Stephanie, Julie, Jolene, and Denise. I cannot express how grateful I am to all of you for taking care of my hands while I pushed a little too hard for a little too long. I am blessed to have you all as part of my care team.

Finally, to my readers: You do me the greatest of honors by reading my books. I appreciate you so very much.

ABOUT THE AUTHOR

Gerri Russell is an award-winning author of historical and contemporary novels, including the Brotherhood of the Scottish Templars series and *Flirting with Felicity*. A two-time recipient of the RWA's Golden Heart Award and winner of the American Title II competition sponsored by *RT Book Reviews* magazine, she's best known for her adventurous, emotionally intense novels set in the thirteenth- and fourteenth-century Scottish Highlands. Before Gerri followed her passion for writing romance novels, she worked as a broadcast journalist, a newspaper reporter, a magazine columnist, a technical writer and editor, and an instructional designer. She lives in Bellevue, Washington, with her husband and children.